The dream team—not!

Loudmouth Lydia, macho Max, peg leg Prairie, and sumo Solano. Talk about the dream team. We had the slowest time of all the relay teams. Big surprise. If you think we're going to exercise, get energized, and rally from behind to win in the end, you've OD'd on Disney. Get real. We didn't kill each other, which was a big disappointment for Max, I think. . . .

"Between bites of every kind of candy imaginable, Jenny provides a glib, fast-paced first-person narration, which is peppered with verbal repartee and humorous asides about her classmates. Peters's writing is smooth and funny."
—*Kirkus Reviews*

REVENGE OF THE
SNOB SQUAD

JULIE ANNE PETERS

SCHOLASTIC INC.

New York Toronto London Auckland Sydney
Mexico City New Delhi Hong Kong

ISBN 0-439-26747-1

12 11 10 9 8 7 6 5 4 3 2   1 2 3 4 5/0

Printed in the U.S.A.   40

First Scholastic printing, December 2000

To Zo Milne,
special teacher, treasured friend

REVENGE OF THE SNOB SQUAD

Chapter 1

If they gave out a World's Worst Whiner Award, Lydia Beals would get it. She was already an official member of the Mickey Mouth Club. Totally obnoxious. And a brown-noser to boot. Nobody at Montrose Middle School could stand Lydia Beals. Including me.

Today Lydia was whining about having P.E. for six weeks straight. I had to agree, even though I didn't say it. Not even Lydia could hate gym class more than me. Mrs. Carpezio, our gym teacher, was off on maternity leave—having triplets, she claimed. Secretly I suspected she'd been bingeing on basketballs. It was real exciting for her but left us with this substitute, Mr. Dietz. Old. Crotchety.

First time I saw him I thought, He's not going to

3

make it across the court without a walker. As I dragged into the gymnasium behind my class, I heard Lydia tell him, "Don't you know that choosing up teams causes permanent psychological damage in children? I should know. My mother's a child psychologist."

We heard this about six times a day.

Mr. Dietz said, "How 'bout if I make you a captain?"

Lydia's jaw jammed in the stuck-open position. "Okay." She beamed.

I dreaded gym anyway, but when Mr. Dietz announced that our school would be participating in a new fitness program, he almost got to scrape my lunch off the freshly lacquered floor. And when he said the first phase was team relay races, I considered leaving him breakfast, too. I wasn't alone. The communal groan could be heard in Pittsburgh. Where is Pittsburgh, anyway?

"Shut the door," Mr. Dietz told me. "Look alive."

I gave him my classic look of the Living Dead. It was a vacant stare perfected after many years of practice.

As usual, the elite cliques immediately separated themselves from the rest of us pond scum. Mr. Dietz blew his whistle, hoping, I guess, to cut through the comas. Good luck.

"Okay, folks, let's choose up teams."

To make myself invisible (which is a laugh if you could see me), I slouched against the tumbling mats in the back. Why delude myself? I always have been, and always will be, the last one picked for any team—sports or academic. Lydia Beals may be called Bealsqueal behind her back, but they call me Lardo Legs to my face.

"Melanie," Lydia called out her first choice. Prize pick for a relay race. Melanie had legs from here to Hong Kong. Where is Hong Kong?

"You gotta be kidding." Melanie tossed her thick lemon locks up over her shoulder. Melanie also had an ego that stretched to Toledo. Where is—oh, forget it.

"Mr. Dietz, do I have to?" she whined. "Ashley said I could be on her team."

Mr. Dietz hemmed. He hawed. Ashley Krupps was the principal's daughter and Dietz knew it. You didn't disappoint the principal's daughter. Not if you wanted to work at Montrose tomorrow.

"Okay, forget Melanie." Lydia saved his scrawny neck. "I'll take Zach Romero." As opposed to the new

Zach whatever-his-name, who was as yet unproven. He'd be picked before me, too. Watch.

"No way, Jose," Zach said. "I'm on Kevin Rooney's team."

The sound of Kevin's name perked me up. I'm deeply in love with Kevin Rooney. Like I have a chance.

"Kevin hasn't even picked yet!" Lydia screeched. She hoisted her hands onto her hips. Through squinty eyes, she threatened the rest of us. Everyone lurched backward a step. Except me, of course.

"I'll go," a raspy voice rose from the sidelines. Pushing off from the brick wall with one army boot, Max McFarland strode across the basketball court. The sea parted to let Max through.

This is an interesting development, I thought. Max McFarland rarely participated in gym class. Only when we played basketball (which was my second most despised sport) or volleyball (a close third). Max was big. Not fat, like me, but solid. Bones of bronze. And tall, at least five ten. Mean, to boot. She scared the bejeezus out of us. Boys included.

Maxine McFarland. The only girl I knew who wore a training bra in second grade.

"Kevin, your pick," the daring Mr. Dietz called

out. Kevin, love of my life, hitched his chin a fraction of an inch. Zach Romero responded. He swaggered up to take his predetermined position behind Kevin.

The last six squad captains made their picks. Then it was Lydia's turn again. "Rachel Cagney," she said.

"Mr. Dietz, Ashley promised I could be on her team, too." Rachel batted her mascara-caked eyelashes at Mr. Dietz. Gag me with an ice cream scoop.

"This isn't fair," Lydia wailed. "I'm the team cap—" Her words got garbled by the stranglehold Max imposed on her neck. The grip and twist caused the top button of Lydia's white lace blouse to pop off. It skittered across the shiny floor, while Max whispered in Lydia's ear.

"What!" Lydia recoiled. She glared at Max. Only for an instant, though. Lydia wasn't stupid. Her tight lips drew tighter. She folded her arms and humphed. "I pick Prairie," she muttered.

My eyebrows arched. Two interesting developments in one day. Spare me the excitement. Apparently Max McFarland planned to lose the race. Prairie Cactus (what a name, huh?) limped across the floor and teetered into place behind Max. If her head was even with Max's elbow, Prairie had grown an inch since lunch.

Even the physically challenged got picked before me. I tried not to let on what torture this was. From my pocket I withdrew a KitKat and unwrapped it.

As teams formed, the throng thinned. The lights dimmed. Finally it was the last round. Oh, the agony. I yearned for a Reese's peanut butter cup. A Snickers. One nub of a soft and chewy super-size Tootsie Roll.

Lydia's final turn. She opened her mouth, then clamped it shut. Twisting her head around, she queried Max. Max considered the crowd, nodded, and handed down her decision in Lydia's ear.

Lydia balked. Apparently she didn't value her life. Max balled a fist. Clucking in disgust, Lydia said, "Okay. Jenny Solano."

What? I jerked awake. Me? My eyes darted around the gym. It's a miracle, I thought. As I waddled my way past the remaining sixth graders to the opposite end, I counted heads. . . . Five, six, seven. For the first time in my life, I wasn't dead last. I was seventh to last.

"Thank you, God," I prayed to the acoustic tile. So this is what it feels like to be among the chosen few.

Chapter 2

Loudmouth Lydia, macho Max, peg leg Prairie, and sumo Solano. Talk about the dream team. We had the slowest time of all the relay teams. Big surprise. If you think we're going to exercise, get energized, and rally from behind to win in the end, you've OD'd on Disney. Get real. We didn't kill each other, which was a big disappointment for Max, I think. After the first heat she asked Mr. Dietz if she could just run all four legs of the race herself. That made Lydia foam at the mouth. Personally I felt it was the only chance we had. If Mr. Dietz promised me the Milky Way, or even a package of them, I couldn't have made it around that track again. Luckily he didn't have to decide because the bell rang.

Mr. Dietz's shrill whistle brought the thundering herd stampeding toward the building to a slow-motion, dust-raising halt. "Since we're going to run relays for two weeks to see how our times improve," he announced, "we'll keep the same squads."

Rats. I was hoping somehow, by default, to end up on Kevin Rooney's team. I wasn't the only one disappointed. Lydia looked like she was going to throw a hyper hissy fit, right there on the gravel, until Max shut her down with sledgehammer eyes. "Good idea, Mr. Dietz." Lydia smiled through clenched teeth. Always the brown-nose.

After school I plopped down in front of the TV with a bag of Cheetos to watch *Oprah*. She's my idol. Oprah says addictions, especially food addictions, are caused by a void in your life. I wasn't sure what my void was. Lately I'd begun to think it was my hamster, Petey, who'd died on Halloween night. His empty cage still sat in my bedroom, haunting me.

Oprah's show today was on mixed marriages. Mentally I replaced the happy couple on stage with Kevin Rooney and me. Major mix: the Blob and the Babe.

Vanessa, my demented sister, crashed in the front door. She clucked her tongue at me in disgust, and I returned the greeting. "Turn it down," she snarled. "I have to practice."

Vanessa was addicted to the clarinet, among other things. I knew what her void was. She was missing a brain.

Dad, who was between jobs and had been for four years now, followed Vanessa in. He juggled a couple of grocery bags on one arm.

"Ahoy, matey," I called to him. "Toss me them thar cookies."

He threw me the bag of Chips Ahoys. While he played Mr. Mom in the kitchen, I turned up the volume on *Oprah*, just to irk Vanessa. It worked. She slammed her door. Dad hollered. I warmed from within.

Dinner was meat loaf and mashed potatoes. My father cooked three things: meat loaf and mashed potatoes, meat loaf and French fries, meat loaf and hash browns. He kidded Mom that he was just a meat and potatoes kind of guy. I think the joke was wearing a little thin. Mom didn't laugh anymore when she got up to nuke a bag of frozen veggies.

"How was school today, Jenny?" she asked, passing me the bowl of green beans.

I passed on the beans. Must leave room for dessert. "Fine."

She sighed. "Could you spare us a few details?"

"Fine and dandy?"

Dad chuckled. I didn't think mentioning the D minus on my math quiz would make for pleasant conversation over dinner. Besides, I was intent on counting. Forty-five, forty-six, forty-seven. Vanessa swallowed. She has this new obsession about chewing every bite of food fifty times before swallowing.

"Uht." I pointed across the table. "That was only forty-nine. A piece of green bean is on its way to your stomach. Better go throw up."

"Jenny!" Mom's hand hit the table.

My hunk of meat loaf jumped off my plate and bounced into my lap.

"May I be excused?" Vanessa asked. She rose from her chair.

Dad said, "You haven't eaten one bite of my meat loaf. And I used a special filler."

"Yeah, rubber," I said.

Vanessa glared at me. "Sorry, I'm just not hungry. Anyway"—she dabbed her chin with a napkin—"I have a lot of practicing to do. The orchestra concert's in like two weeks, you know? I'll never learn the Mozart in time."

Mom sighed. "Go ahead." Her eyes didn't even trail Vanessa out; they just zeroed in on me.

"What?" I asked.

"If you can't say something nice to your sister, don't say anything at all."

"Fine by me. It's going to get real quiet around here. Mind if I bring my CD player to dinner?"

In answer, Mom's lips grew taut. She deferred to Dad. Dad smiled at me. "You know, Jen, your birthday's coming up in a couple of weeks. Why don't you invite some friends over for a party?"

I just looked at him. Then I looked at Mom and back at him. "What? And share the cake?"

Dad laughed. Mom shot him with poison-packed pupils, and he changed the laugh to a cough.

"You never talk about school or your friends or anything that's going on in your life," Mom said. "You have no extracurricular activities, and when I try to interest you in things, you turn up your nose."

"You mean that gymnastics club?" I scoffed. "Get real. Now, if you could get me into sumo wrestling—"

Mom continued as if I hadn't even spoken. "And after last term's grades . . ." She shook her head.

"We're concerned about you, Jenny. Very concerned."

My head dropped. For some reason tears welled in my eyes. It wasn't like we didn't have this conversation once a week, at least.

"I'm thinking about sending you to a psychologist."

"What!" That shot my head up. It almost ripped right off my spinal cord and splattered against the fridge.

"We think you need professional help with"—she swallowed hard—"your problem."

I saw Dad blush.

I gasped as both hands flew up to cover my head. "Who told you? Vanessa? That snitch. She's been counting hairs in the brush again, hasn't she?"

Mom looked confused. "Told us what?"

"About my problem. About . . ."—my voice lowered—"my premature hair loss."

Dad couldn't help it. He burst out laughing. Mother was not amused.

Chapter 3

The next day I zoned through language arts and math. Usually I can make my mind a total blank, but today I couldn't stop thinking. About what Mom had said. A psychologist. A shrink. A head fed. Was I really nuts? If I was, I wanted to be cashews. Then another thought barreled through my brain. What if the psychologist Mom picked turned out to be Lydia's mother? I glanced over at Lydia. At her empty desk. She was up at Mrs. Jonas's desk, squealing (literally) on Ashley for grabbing her book and losing her place during silent reading. Lydia was pathetic. This was my role model?

During gym, while the teams were supposed to be loosening up with calisthenics and stretching exercises, my team congregated at the bleachers. Lydia plopped down Indian-style underneath the seats and yanked a paperback out of her pocket. Some trashy romance novel. With a picture like that on the cover, you can bet it didn't come from our school media center.

Max perched above Lydia on the risers, picking the scab off her elbow from an apparent stab wound. As I clomped up, Prairie Cactus smiled demurely at me from her bleacher seat two rows below Max. I plopped on the row between them.

"So, what's our strategy today?" I said to no one in particular.

"Huh?" Max grunted behind me.

My Mars Bar had gone gooey in my pocket. Rats. I slurped the soupy slime out of the wrapper. "Our strategy. How do we intend to show up these losers and make the best time?"

From underneath us, a howl like a sick hyena rose up. Lydia had the most obnoxious laugh. Behind me, Max blew a puff of air out between her lips. Prairie said, "B-b-better leave me out. I-I'm not a very good runner."

Understatement of the century.

"Everyone runs today," Max said. "I'll take the first leg."

"Great," I said. "After you finish with it, could I gnaw on the bone?"

Prairie covered her mouth and tittered. Hey, encouragement. "Unless anyone has an objection," I continued, "I prefer the last leg. The anchor? I think I can drag us down. Get it? Anchor? Drag?"

"I think I sh-should run the anchor l-leg," Prairie said. She lifted her right pant leg to show us her fake foot.

Lydia gasped. Max snorted. A smile tugged the corners of my lips.

"What happened to your foot?" Lydia said as she sashayed around the end of the bleacher box.

Max and I both shot Lydia dead with eye bullets, even though I was curious, too.

"B-birth defect," Prairie said. "N-no big deal. But I can't run too good."

"Well, *I* can run," Lydia said. "I still hold the record in the hundred-yard dash from third grade."

Dead silence.

"Look in the trophy case at Greenlee Elementary if you don't believe me."

I almost said, "There must have been an epidemic that year—a lot of kids out sick." Maybe I did say it.

Lydia dog-eared the page of her book. "I'll run the

anchor. If no one has an objection, that is." She looked at me.

Max made sounds like she was going to spit a loogie on Lydia. I twisted around and discouraged her with a grimace. She swallowed it, reluctantly.

"You jocks fight it out." Max stood. The vibrating bleachers rattled my teeth as she tromped down past me. "See you at the starting line."

Like sheep led to slaughter, Prairie and I followed Max. Lydia caught up to me. "Since I'm team captain, I should decide the order we run in. Don't you think?"

Max stopped dead in her tracks. She whirled on Lydia. A detectable tremor raced from Lydia's limp hair bow to her Keds rubber guards. "Why don't you run the first leg," she said meekly to Max.

"Wise decision," I muttered under my breath.

"Jenny, you're second."

I clucked.

"What?" Lydia huffed. "I'm running the anchor. It's our only chance."

At what? I thought. Less than total humiliation? I clucked again. Just to be ornery. Lydia exhaled a sigh of exasperation.

"Prairie, you run third," she said. "And for heaven's sake, don't anyone drop the baton again."

"Like y-y-you did y-yesterday?" Prairie piped up. I choked. Max smirked.

Lydia ignored us. "All right, team. Let's show these loggerheads how it's done."

Max rolled her eyes at me. I was beginning to like this girl.

"It's not a race," I reminded everyone.

Lydia just stared at the field, eyes narrowed. She was determined—you had to give her that.

We'd reached the track, where Max approached the starting line and did a deep knee bend. Meanwhile, I freed a fire stick from my back pocket. Lydia glared at me. "You're not going to eat that now, are you?"

I stared at Lydia, then down at the fire stick. With a heartsick sigh, I stuck it back in my pocket. "Guess not." To myself I added, Dad always said it's not polite to eat and run.

We ran eight seconds slower than the day before. Not bad, I thought. Nobody got hurt.

Ashley Krupps approached us after the relays, no doubt to tell us we were lousy, which we already knew. "What do you want?" Lydia snarled.

I hate Ashley Krupps. Hate her to her rotten apple core. I have my reasons. And it's not because she's the principal's daughter, or because she's fat like me and doesn't care. No one ever makes fun of Ashley

19

Krupps. Probably because she has the power to get them expelled on a whim. I thought Lydia should be careful.

Ashley said, "Our squad decided, since we're going to keep the same teams, that we should make up team names."

Melanie drew up alongside Ashley. She swabbed nonexistent sweat off her forehead. "Our name is the Neon Nikes," she sang in a singsong.

"Oh, brother," Lydia muttered.

Really, I agreed.

Their two other team members appeared, like right off the cover of *Preteen Queen*. Rachel Cagney and Fayola K. No one with English as their native tongue could pronounce Fayola's K.'s last name. There weren't any vowels in it. Fayola had a personal vendetta against me because I once referred to her as Fayola Crayola. I think she thought it was a racial slur, but all I meant was that she used very colorful language.

"Oh, damn," she said. "I broke a nail. Damn, damn, damn!"

See?

"James Martinez's team is the Oakland Raiders," Rachel said.

"Original," I replied between licks of fire stick.

Lydia snorted.

"What's Kevin Rooney's name?" Melanie asked Rachel. She was in love with him, too. Which made me despise her.

"I don't know," Rachel said. "They're still arguing about it." We all looked over. Fisticuffs were about to break out between the boys.

"How about the Rooney Tunes?" I hollered over.

Ashley, Melanie, Rachel, and Fayola all made the same face at me. So that's what they did in the rest room for twelve hours at a stretch. Fayola said, "You're real friggin' funny, Solano." She didn't say friggin'.

"Thank you." No one ever accused me of bad manners.

"So, anyway"— Ashley started to walk away — "that's what the *rest* of us are doing." She addressed me personally on her way past. "Not that *you* should feel like *you're* included."

A retort formed on my tongue, then dribbled off. It had too much of Fayola's colorful language to voice out loud.

Out of nowhere Lydia announced, "We're the Snob Squad."

The Neon Nikes skidded to a group halt. They exchanged glances like . . . like they wished they'd have thought of the name. We stared at Lydia like she was lights out, long gone.

Max rolled her eyes at me. I rolled mine back.

After the Nikes left, we all turned to Lydia. Max said what we were thinking. "The Snob Squad?"

Lydia hooked a hunk of hair behind her ear. "Why not?" she said.

Max looked at me. I looked at Prairie. Prairie shrugged. "W-why not?"

A million reasons. None of which I was willing to share if they didn't already know.

"The Snob Squad," Max repeated. "I like it."

Lydia beamed.

See? Others need professional help a lot more than me.

Chapter 4

There's this saying: Birds of a feather flock together. I don't know how we qualified as birds exactly, but we started flocking. Far as I could tell, the only thing the four of us, the Snob Squad, had in common was that we were the most unpopular people in school.

I first noticed this flocking phenomenon at lunch the next day. My whole school life I'd always eaten lunch alone, off at the most remote cafeteria table under a flickering fluorescent bulb. Now Max, Lydia, and Prairie joined me. It was weird. The feel of other people, the sounds of group chewing.

Lydia blabbered on and on about how she hated Ashley Krupps. How Ashley was a stuck-up liar and a slut, a spoiled brat juvenile delinquent, et cetera, et cetera. I relished her rage. It reaffirmed my feelings.

Lydia was still steaming from the incident that morning. After we were all settled in class and ready for roll call, Lydia opened her desk and screamed. Inside was a dead bull snake. Fresh roadkill; the floppy body was still warm. You should've seen Lydia. Major conniption. Anyway, since Ashley was laughing at Lydia the loudest, Lydia assumed she'd done it. She probably did. She was always tormenting Lydia. Doing things just to make her scream. Naturally everyone thought it was a hoot. I would've too, if someone other than Ashley had been responsible.

We all tried to console Lydia. Except Max. She said, "Could I have the snake?"

Lydia just looked at her. "I don't have it. I don't know what happened to it." She shuddered.

Max clucked her tongue. Major disappointment.

After lunch Prairie had to go finish some kind of IQ test. Lydia, Max, and I wandered back to the clown target behind the baseball field. The clown target was the PTA's pet project last year. It was supposed to stop kids from throwing snowballs at each other by eliminating the temptation. Yeah, right. Winter was a heavy referral season at Montrose.

Max scooped up a dirt clod from the outfield and slung it through Bozo's gaping mouth. Lydia and I balanced on the chain-link fence in front of the dugout to watch. Okay, Lydia balanced. I buttressed.

"She's weird," Lydia whispered to me.

Look who's talking, I thought. I replied, "Who isn't? You want a Smarties?"

"Sure."

I handed her a roll. We unwrapped our candy in unison. While we sucked on the pellets, we continued to watch Max. She was gathering a crowd. Mostly guys who secretly admired her arm, I suspected.

"Here comes Prairie," Lydia said, pointing. "She must've finished her test early."

Prairie was limping out the A wing door. She scanned the playground. When she saw us, she waved and started over. To get to where we were, she had to walk through the crowd watching Max. Just like always, it happened. Whenever Prairie Cactus passed by a group, especially boys, she became a target. She was fingered and poked, pushed and prodded. Teased with cries of "Ow! Ooh! Prickly!"

As she hobbled by the onlookers in the field, it started up. "Ow, ooh, ouch, ooch." Max paused mid-sling. She spun on the crowd. There was one final

"Ouch" as Prairie emerged. Max charged forward and grabbed the shirtfront of the boy who'd last poked Prairie. "What'd you say?" she asked him.

He sneered. "I said ouch." He looked to the kid beside him for support. The kid backed off. Funny how your best friend in the world will desert you in a moment of crisis.

"You must have ESP," Max said. She hauled off and punched him in the stomach. He squealed and staggered backward. "Who else said ouch?" Max held up a fist.

No other confessions were forthcoming. The crowd dispersed, fast.

My palms drew together. In slow syncopation I clapped, paused, clapped, paused . . .

Lydia picked up the rhythm. Wheeling toward us, Max's face registered . . . nothing. Or something; something impossible to read. If she'd had an Uzi, she might have gunned us down, like the dumb smart-offs we were. After a minute, one corner of her lip curled up and she bowed. Now that's class.

When Mr. Dietz called the Snob Squad to the starting line that afternoon, Max led the way. From the sidelines we cheered. Our hero.

The Nikes just looked at us. Everyone did. It made us cheer louder. I even whistled through the gap in my two front teeth. Funny how you'll do stupid stuff in a group you'd never do alone. Mr. Dietz blew his whistle to start the time trials.

Max was breathing hard as she rounded the track to hand the baton off to Prairie. For an instant we were ahead of yesterday's time. Lydia's new strategy for the day was to switch me and Prairie. Prairie ran second; I was third. Don't ask me why. Lydia was captain.

Prairie limped around as best she could, but by the time she crossed the finish line three days later, we were behind again. If Lydia thought I was going to improve our time, she was denser than I figured.

"Good try," I heard Max say to Prairie as I took off like an earthquake. When I thundered over the finish line, sweating like a roast pig, Max said, "Good race, Solano."

I sneered at the insult. Funny though, Max seemed sincere. I felt better. Less like Flubber burning rubber. A few feet behind us the Nikes' heads were drawn together. They were plotting something—you could smell it. Mostly what I smelled was Melanie's perfume. P.U. How could Kevin Rooney stand to be within sniffing distance of her without hyperventilating? Myself, I've always considered the fragrance of deep, dark chocolate to be irresistibly appealing.

Lydia charged around the last curve, running, as she did, like a knock-kneed duck. She had to be related to Daffy, no kidding. Her lack of style was glaring, too, since she was all alone on the track. Someone, Fayola I think, said, "Quack," to mock Lydia, and Max's head nearly propelled off her neck trying to catch who it was. I visualized it: one army boot to Fayola's front teeth. Crunch. Talk about colorful.

As Lydia came flat-footing toward home, the Nikes advanced. Suddenly Lydia went flying. She crossed the finish line facefirst. An anguished yowl rose up from the dirt, loud enough to roust the roadkill in Rangoon. Where is Rangoon?

I lumbered over to Lydia, Max zooming past me. "You okay?" She yanked Lydia to her feet by the waistband of her stretch pants. Prairie retrieved Lydia's glasses and handed them to her.

Lydia's nose was bleeding, and her palms were embedded with gravel. She shoved her glasses on. "My new pants!" she screeched.

Sure enough, the knees of Lydia's green and yellow flowered pants were shredded. A blessing in disguise, I thought. "Someone tripped me," Lydia snuffled.

Max's spine went rigid.

"It's true," I said, staring at Lydia's knees. Without warning, my vision blurred. All that blood was making me woozy. Either that or my blood sugar level was dangerously low, since I hadn't eaten in an hour. Taking a deep breath, I added, "I won't name names, but it was Ashley Krupps. I saw her stick her foot out." You couldn't miss those size twelve, shocking pink Reeboks.

Max lunged for Ashley, fist clenched.

"It wasn't me," Ashley said, cowering behind Melanie. Max threatened Melanie with her other fist.

"I didn't do it," she whimpered.

"None of us did anything." Ashley regained her composure. "She just fell. Lydia's a klutz." The Neon Nikes all nodded in unison.

Beside me, Max growled. I held her back. Tried to.

"All right, break it up." Dauntless Dietz rushed in at the last moment. "You, go to the office and get cleaned up. The rest of you girls take your starting positions." He raised his whistle to his withered lips.

"But Mr. Dietz," Lydia wailed, "Ashley tripped me! Aren't you going to do anything about it?"

He looked from Lydia to Ashley and gulped. "Shake hands and make up."

"For what?" Ashley said. "I didn't do anything. She's a whiner. Ask anyone."

I hoped he wouldn't. "Come on, Lydia." I took her arm. "He isn't going to do anything. He can't. He has to keep working so he can get Social Security." I glared at him, daring him to deny it.

He didn't.

Max, Prairie, and I trailed the sniffling, hobbling Lydia to the nurse. Someone behind us said under her breath, "Quack." I recognized that voice. I won't name names. Max stiffened. She didn't turn around. She just balled both fists at her sides and seethed, "You know what this means."

I took a stab. "Their goose is cooked?"

Between clenched teeth, Max snarled one word: "War."

Chapter 5

Lined up along the length of the army cot in the school clinic, we watched while Lydia got her temperature taken. It's a state law or something that even if you go to the nurse bleeding to death from a pencil up the nose, you have to have your temperature taken. After sticking the thermometer down Lydia's throat, the nurse disappeared. We heard her giggling at some crack Principal Krupps made out in the hall.

Max muttered, "Solano said it first. We need a strategy."

"I said that? When did I say that?"

"We need to set up a command post. Some place underground. A secret headquarters."

Max, I thought, you've been watching too many Schwarzenneger movies.

"What about Ms. M-Milner's room?" Prairie said. She sat crouched next to me, elbows on knees. "N-no one goes there."

Unless they have to.

"Forget it." Lydia pulled the plastic thermometer out of her mouth. "I'm not setting foot in the special ed room." She blinked at Prairie. "No offense." The thermometer slid back into her mouth.

I wondered what the human temperature was at the moment of strangulation. From the look on Max's face, she was wondering the same thing.

"N-none taken," Prairie said, sparing Lydia's larynx.

Prairie spent most mornings in Ms. Milner's PC lab. I'm not sure what *PC* stood for—I didn't think it was *Politically Correct*. Most everyone referred to it as the retard room.

"We need a place away from school," Max continued. "At someone's house." She looked at me.

"Don't look at me. I take the bus." Which was another trauma I'd be dealing with well into adulthood.

Max arched an eyebrow at Prairie. "I have s-six brothers," Prairie said.

We all groaned.

Eyes focused on Lydia. She removed the thermometer again. "My mother doesn't allow me to have friends over when she's not home. Anyway, I go to day care after school."

Day care? I said what everyone else was thinking. "Day care?"

If the blood rushing to her face was any indication, Lydia's temperature shot up a hundred degrees.

"We'll meet at my house then," Max said. "You know where the old burned-out firehouse is?"

Everyone knew where the old burned-out firehouse was. Last year's most talked about news event. And the name in the news was Max McFarland. She'd been expelled for a month because someone reported her smoking there.

"I live right behind it," Max said.

"In the dump?" The thermometer fell out of Lydia's mouth.

Max glared. "It's not a dump. It's a junk car lot. My brother buys old cars and fixes them up. That's his business. He sells hard-to-find car parts."

They *would* be hard to find in that jalopy junkyard, I thought.

Max added, "You can come to my house with me after school today." It wasn't a request. She twisted her head toward me. "My brother will drive you home afterward."

We were all expecting it, the whine, the excuse, the drawn-out explanation. The three of us looked at Lydia.

"I'll have to call my mother at work," is all she said. Shock. She retrieved the thermometer from under the sink and blew it off.

We got up to follow Lydia to the phone. On the way out, Prairie took the thermometer from Lydia and squinted at it. "N-n-normal," she pronounced.

"Must be defective," I muttered. Max slugged my shoulder. Good thing I'm padded.

We rendezvoused at the clown target after school. Before leaving the school yard, Max flung one last dirt clod at Bozo. Direct hit, right between the eyes.

Max led us down Erie Avenue, through the alley, and in between a row of decrepit apartment houses. The sign said LUXURY LIVING.

"Which one's Donald Trump's?" I asked.

Lydia laughed. Max and Prairie didn't get it, I guess.

As we passed by the burned-out firehouse, we all gaped, and gulped. None of us dared look at Max. At the junkyard — excuse me, Used Auto Parts Estab-

lishment — we picked our way through the cata-
combs of car corpses back to a ramshackle house,
nearly camouflaged in the rubble.

"I'm home!" Max bellowed as she hurled open the
back door. No one answered. It was dim in the
kitchen, even though it was still broad daylight at
three-thirty in the afternoon and the overhead light
was on. The walls were dingy, covered in striped,
mousy wallpaper, stained and peeling at the corners.
I wouldn't normally notice wallpaper except there
was movement behind one strip over by the stove.
Maybe it was my imagination, or maybe this was the
original roach motel.

"I said I'm home!" Max's husky voice, raised in
volume, flattened my ears.

"Keep it down, toad breath." A taller, hairier
version of Max emerged from the darkened doorway. He wore blue jeans, no shirt, shaggy beard. He
looked like he'd just got out of bed. "Mom's channel-
ing," he said, raking fingers through his snarled hair.

Beside me I felt Max tense. "These are my friends."
She nodded to us. "Solano, Lyd, and Prayer. My
brother, Scuzz-Gut." They traded sneers.

"Don't you want to know who died?" he said
to Max.

"Not really." She flung her backpack through the

open doorway into the living room. I've always wanted to do that—announce my arrival home by pitching my backpack through the door. With my luck I'd bust a lamp.

"Some old lady's great-aunt from Cleveland," he told her anyway, scratching his chest. "She wants to find out where the old bag buried all her money."

I wanted to ask, but the look Max shot me said, "Don't." A thought flashed through my head: Where is Cleveland? Then another one: I wish I lived here. The most unusual thing that ever happened at my house was the cable TV cutting out.

Even though we were squeezed in the kitchen tight as a Twinkies twelve-pack, Scuzz-Gut wrenched open the refrigerator and pulled out a beer. Max said to him, "Mind if we hang out in the old VW van?"

"The Peacemobile?" He popped the top.

"We won't wreck anything."

"Better not. That microbus is a classic. I had a guy in looking at it yesterday. He might be interested."

"In what?" Max said sarcastically. "The rusted-out frame? The battery cavity? The cracked engine block?"

She rolled her eyes at me. I was impressed with her knowledge of automobiles. I knew tires, steering wheel, tape player. . . .

Her brother wedged by us toward the living room door. "Just don't contaminate it with cooties." He shivered all over.

I looked at Max. She made some hand gesture at her brother's back I'd never seen before. I stored it in my repertoire for Vanessa.

"Come on." She led us out the door toward the microbus. "Oh, and Scuzz-Gut," she hollered back through the torn screen. "Don't get drunk. You have to drive Solano home later."

From the doorway, across the dim kitchen and through the torn back screen, his eyes met mine. I could tell he was thrilled. He guzzled half the can. Be still, my stomach.

The Peacemobile seemed a strange place to set up a command post for war. But it was, in a word, awesome. My dad would say cool, hip, groovy. The exterior—the part that wasn't rusted out—had once been plastered with hundreds, maybe thousands, of peace symbols. You know, the circle with the upside-down Y inside? All sizes, shapes, colors.

"You got anything to eat?" Max said as she yanked open the squeaky side panel to the microbus and motioned us in.

The magic word. I scrounged in my backpack. Yikes. My supplies were dwindling. We'd depleted a

lot of the inventory at lunch. Feeling around, I noticed a lump in my front jeans pocket. Voilà. I held
up half a package of Bit-o-Honey.

"Great." Max grabbed it. "Sit." She waved us to a
saggy, flowered couch.

As I sat, a spring ripped through the upholstery
and bit my butt. I screamed and Prairie giggled.
Lydia lowered herself cautiously, flicking a hunk of
sponge to the floor.

Max ripped off one segment of Bit-o-Honey and
passed around the last three squares. "All right," she
said, flopping into a pistachio green beanbag chair
across from us. "We have to attack tomorrow. Let
'em know we won't put up with any more of this
crap."

"Wait a minute," Lydia interrupted. "I'm the captain of this squad. I should be in charge."

Max lounged back. She crossed one army boot
over her knee. "Okay." She bit into her Bit-o-Honey.
"You're in charge."

Lydia cleared her throat. She stood. Clasping her
hands behind her back, she began to pace. About
four steps. That was all the room she had. "We have
to strike soon." She pivoted in place. "The sooner the
better."

"Tomorrow," Max garbled.

Lydia silenced her with a look. Dangerous move, I thought. Lydia continued, "They're going to have to pay for these pants, number one."

I groaned. "Look, the only way to really get at these airheads is to give them a taste of their own medicine. Taunt them. Torment them. Humiliate them in public." I said to Lydia, "Like Ashley does to you a hundred times a day."

"Excellent." Lydia spun on me. "What's your plan, Solano?"

I balked. "I don't have a plan. You're in charge, remember?"

Lydia turned to Max. Max shrugged.

It was quiet in the van for a few minutes, so quiet you could hear metal rusting. Out of nowhere, a tiny voice piped up, "I-I-I have an idea."

All eyes locked on Prairie. She told us what it was. I think the Bit-o-Honey may have given her the inspiration, while it just gave the rest of us cavities.

Besides being brilliant, Prairie's plan was devious, demented, and dirty. We loved it.

Before the meeting broke up, we made a pact. If one of us goes down, we all go down. We stacked hands on it. The next day I wished I hadn't.

Chapter 6

When I got home, Mom met me at the door. "Who was that?" she asked, watching Scuzz-Gut spew gravel as he ripped away from the curb. Miraculously he'd managed not to total the car on the ride home. Max came along, thank God. She still scared me, but her brother reminded me of this serial killer my dad once told me about. Jeffrey Dahmer. He chopped up his victims and stored their body parts in the fridge. For a year after that, I shivered every time I opened the fridge, and not from the cold. Something in the way Scuzz-Gut eyed me and drooled sent chills down my spine.

"Max and Scuzz —" I stopped. "Just a ride. Where's Dad?"

Mom closed the door behind me, still staring down

the block where the smoking Camaro squealed around the corner. "He had a job interview this afternoon."

"Oh, yeah? Who with?"

"He didn't say. He did say you called and told him you had a meeting after school."

I tossed my backpack on the couch and flopped down next to it. "That's right. You'll be glad to know I've joined a club."

Mom perched on the La-Z-Boy next to me. She folded her hands in her lap. "Really? What kind of club?"

"Oh, a girls club. You know."

"No, I don't know. What's the name of this club?"

"The, uh—" I yawned. "SnobgarbleSquadgarble." She still looked dubious. "We do good deeds, make pledges, that kind of stuff. A girls club."

"Do you sell cookies?" Mom smiled.

I snapped my fingers. "Now there's an idea."

Her face sobered again. "Jenny—"

"And," I went on, "you'll be glad to know that my problem is under control. My class is involved in a fitness program until the end of the year. There're rigorous workouts every day. No doubt I'll drop twenty, twenty-five pounds without even trying." I grinned. "So, you can forget about the shrink."

She winced at the word. Not hard enough. "I already made an appointment," she said.

I freaked. "Cancel it."

She stood. "I couldn't get you in until the twenty-first, though. Can you believe how booked up these people are? I can't imagine there are that many kids with"—she blinked away—"problems."

"Major problems, Mom. Major. You don't want to burden them with my piddly stuff. What's a few extra pounds when people are slitting their wrists, smoking dope, driving without a license—"

Just then Vanessa came tearing out of her room. "Mom, can you take me down to Milton's Music? My last reed just split."

Mom sighed. "Sure," she said.

Wait a minute, I wanted to scream. Remember me? This vital discussion we're having about my life? "Really, Mom. You can cancel the appointment." I pushed to my feet.

"I don't think so." She grabbed her purse.

Right there I suffered a severe emotional trauma. I lost my appetite. Vanessa got the aftershock. On her way past me I said, "Gee, those jeans are getting a little tight across the butt."

She screeched to a stop.

Mom snapped, "Jennifer!"

"Oops." I covered my mouth. "Not nice. I forgot."

Vanessa twisted around. "Are they?" She met my eyes.

What could I say? With my thumb and index finger, I zipped my lip.

"Jenny!" Mom yelled again. To Vanessa she said, "They look fine."

Vanessa sprinted back to her room. "I'm going to change."

Mom turned to me. If looks could fry, I'd be deep fat.

I couldn't wait to get out of the house the next morning. Dad didn't get the job, whatever it was, so he and Mom had a huge argument in the basement. They'd been going at it down there a lot lately, like we couldn't hear. Dinner was total silence. Breakfast, too. My two favorite times of the day, ruined. Add to that watching Vanessa cut every Cheerio in half *before* she chewed it fifty times—hello? *Who* needs a shrink?

The promise of gym class got me through the morning, because today we implemented the Prairie Plan. Yee-haw.

"All right, Solano, give it to me," Max said, extending her hand. We were huddled behind the bleachers, psyching ourselves up. Some might say acting like retards.

"Hold it." Lydia crushed herself between us. "This is my revenge. I get to do it."

Max sagged visibly. She really wanted the honor. With a heavy heart, she dropped her arm.

"Be sure to get it on real thick," Max grumbled. She trailed Lydia to the running track while Prairie and I formed the daring duo at the rear.

"I know. I'm not a total idiot," Lydia said over her shoulder.

"Just half a one," I muttered. Prairie giggled. Max smirked.

We watched Lydia tuck the ammunition into the stretch band of her pants and pull her blouse out to cover it. Real deceptive. It looked like she'd grown a spinal tap. On me the bulge would've dissolved into all my layers of blubber. Maybe I should've claimed the honor.

We asked Dingy Dietz if we could run first. You know, to get the agony out of the way. We needed to be done with our race for the Prairie Plan to begin.

Max lined up for the first leg.

Mr. Dietz set his stopwatch. "Get ready, set, go!" He blew his whistle to start the first heat.

From the sidelines, we whooped a war cry.

We ran a perfect race. Perfectly awful. Max was okay on her leg. But about halfway around the track I slowed to a walk. Why work up a sweat? I figured.

Max seemed miffed. "You could at least try," she said as I jumped backward over the finish line, twirling the baton in the air before handing it off to Prairie. "At least Prayer tries." She motioned to the track, where Prairie Cactus dragged up a dust storm with her bum foot.

Prayer, I repeated to myself. That fits. As in, You know she doesn't have one, Max. Nevertheless, next time I'd trot, at least. For some reason, I wanted Max's approval. Craved it. Maybe because my life depended on it.

Max cheered Prairie on. Her enthusiasm was contagious. Behind me, Lydia said, "I can't wait to see their faces. This is going to be so sweet." She beamed. I beamed back. For once, she was right.

Finally the moment we'd been waiting for. Prairie dragged over the finish line. "Good job." Max clapped Prairie on the back as Lydia bounded away on the last leg.

"Really good." I added my praise.

Prairie's eyes sparkled. "Th-thanks," she wheezed.

Lydia trudged around the track. It took her an ice age. "Go! Run! Atta girl, L.B." Max clapped and cheered. Prairie and I picked up the beat. Out of the bleachers a faint yet distinctive sound drifted down: "Quack. Quack."

Max stopped cheering. Deep in her throat, she growled. Prairie and I exchanged terrified glances and stepped back a couple of feet.

At the far end of the track, Lydia shifted the baton to her right hand. That was my cue. "Oh, my stomach," I moaned real loud. "I think I'm going to be sick." Face contorted, I stumbled over toward Fayola on the first riser of the bleachers, and wretched. She screamed. Everyone turned to look.

I burped. "Ah, much better. Must have been those burritos from lunch." I bounced a fist off my stomach. Disgusting, I know.

Fayola torched me with her eyes. The class resumed whatever they'd been doing — sleeping, molting, laughing at Lydia.

"We'd better get lined up for our race," Ashley said. She stepped daintily down the bleachers. Her mule team followed. As she passed me she said, "Sick."

I wanted to trip her so bad, but it wasn't part of Prairie's plan.

The second heat of runners was rousting themselves from their nap when Lydia finally flat-footed over the finish line. She crouched, catching her breath, or pretending to, as Ashley waddled up and stuck out a hand. "Baton, please."

Here's what was *supposed* to happen. The Prairie Plan. Lydia would plop the baton in Ashley's hand as she sprinted over the finish line. Ashley would run her leg then hand off to Fayola—or try to. "It's all sticky!" Ashley would wail. "It's . . . it's covered with glue."

"Not glue," Lydia would say at my side.

"Honey," we'd jump in. "A little bit o' honey." We'd emphasize the play on words. Then we'd all lapse into hyena hysterics.

Unfortunately the Prairie Plan bombed. About halfway around the track the lid on the honey bear bottle worked itself loose. Probably as a result of Lydia's hammering flat feet on the gravel. Honey dribbled down the rear of her pants. Then the bottle slipped loose and rolled down Lydia's left leg, lodging in the elastic cuff at her ankle.

By the time Lydia limped across the finish line, her left foot had collected about a yard of sand, and her red Keds were oozing amber. All down her orange pants it was wet and sticky. Everyone was pointing and laughing, like she'd done the unthinkable.

Lydia's eyes welled with tears.

"It's okay, Lyd," I tried to console her on the way to the girls' rest room. "Could've happened to any of us." Thank God I didn't get the honor.

"We j-just didn't think it through," Prairie said.

"Now these pants are ruined, too!" Lydia cried. "And so are my new shoes." She wailed. Prairie patted her on the back. We all exchanged sympathetic grimaces.

"This is Krupps's fault," Max said. "Now she's *really* going to get it."

I wasn't exactly sure how Lydia's icky sticky situation could be blamed on Ashley Krupps. But any excuse to get back at her was okay by me.

Chapter $\boxed{7}$

As we settled into the Peace-mobile, it occurred to me that we all had it in for Ashley Krupps. I'd gone to school with her since first grade. We'd never been what you'd call friends. One fat girl alone is bad enough; two fat girls together would be asking for double trouble. We'd always avoided each other. Until last year. Until ... the incident.

"Why does Ashley p-pick on you so b-bad?" Prairie asked Lydia. "I th-thought you were friends."

Lydia clenched her teeth. "At the beginning of the year we were," she said.

I remembered that. They used to eat lunch to-gether, hang out by the bleachers at recess, and cheer while the eighth-grade football team ran laps. Like either of them had a chance.

"At least I thought we were friends," Lydia went on. "Until she found Fayola." Her eyes went dead. "Ashley invited me to a birthday party for Fayola. A surprise party. She said a bunch of seventh and eighth graders were coming. I was really excited because it was the first part—I mean, because it was a boy-girl party. My mom bought me a new dress and everything. It was really beautiful. Then I show up at the time and place on the invitation, and when the door opens I yell, 'Surprise!' Guess what? There was no party. The address Ashley gave me was Kevin Rooney's house. He was home with a couple of guys watching videos. I guess Ashley told them she was sending over a surprise." Lydia's lips quivered. "I was it."

"Oh, man," Max said.

"How m-mean," Prairie said.

"Could I have the address?" I said.

Lydia looked at me. "I don't have it. I burned the invitation. Which is what I'd like to do to Ashley Krupps if I could."

Max said, "Let's firebomb her house."

Was she kidding? Of course she was kidding. I think.

Lydia's eyes lit up. "Okay. When?"

"Now, wait a minute," I said. "I hate her, too, but I don't want to kill her." Which wasn't totally true.

"I do," Max muttered.

We all turned to her. "What'd she do to you?" Lydia asked.

Max removed the baseball cap from her head and ran a hand through her flattened hair. "She got me suspended."

When Max didn't elaborate, Prairie said, "H-how?"

Max exhaled. "She's the one who told the cops I was smoking at the firehouse. She swore she saw me there right before the fire started."

Lydia inhaled audibly. "Were you?"

Max growled at her. "Of course not. I don't smoke." She added in a smaller voice, "At least I don't anymore. Ashley's the one who set it. I saw her there with a bunch of her groupies after school that day, smoking. And she knows I saw her."

"Why didn't you turn her in?" Lydia said.

"Yeah, right." Max snorted. "Like anyone'd believe me over her. You know how *that* works."

We sure did.

"At least you g-got out of school for a m-month." Prairie smiled.

"True." Max smirked. "It wasn't all bad."

"She's such a j-jerk," Prairie said.

"What's she done to you, Prairie?" I asked.

"Nothing." Her eyes fell. "Well . . . when I first moved here, w-we were in youth group at church together. The first day, after I g-got introduced, Ashley poked me and s-said, 'Ooh, p-prickly.' "

"She started that?" I couldn't believe it. Yes, I could. It was Ashley all over. And a cruel taunt like that would spread like a prairie wildfire, which it did.

"What about you, Jenny? You seem to hate her the most," Lydia said.

"Me?" I gulped. How could they know how much I hated Ashley Krupps? How I thought about getting back at her every day of my life? How I wanted to hurt her, bad. Without warning, tears filled my eyes.

Lydia wrapped an arm around my shoulder. "It must be really horrible."

I nodded.

There was a long, agonizing moment when I couldn't speak, when I could hardly breathe. Finally Max said, "She can't talk about it, okay? What's important is, we've got to figure out a way to get back at Krupps. I say firebomb."

"Jenny's right," Lydia said. "We don't want to kill her. Just torture her psychologically. Scar her for life, like she has us." She handed me a Kleenex.

Eventually I got myself under control and said, "We need to figure out the ultimate humiliation." I blew my nose. "We should be able to do that. We've all been there."

"Right." Lydia curled up in her corner of the couch. "Something totally degrading."

"Th-that she'll never forget."

Lydia said, "What's the most horrifying experience you can ever imagine happening to you? Besides being in the same room with Ashley Krupps."

We snorted. Prairie piped up, "Dyeing your hair red and having it c-come out g-green."

We all turned.

"My c-cousin dyed her hair once, and it turned g-green. And she's not even a p-punker."

"Eeoooh." Lydia made a face. "I'd give a month's allowance to see Ashley Krupps with green hair."

Max shot to her feet. "Wait here." She clomped out the door.

"Is she going to get the firebomb kit?" I asked.

Lydia elbowed me, smiling. Sobering fast, she said, "She scares me. Does she scare you?"

"Nah," I lied.

We all stared out the door after Max. Lydia broke the trance. "Got anything to eat, Jenny?" she said.

I proffered my stash. A bag of Keebler fudge stripe cookies I was saving for just such an occasion.

Crunching into one, Prairie said, "Y-your pants don't look t-too bad, Lydia."

Lydia blotted her thigh with her thumb. "They're still sticky. I should make Ashley Krupps wash them. That's it. Let's stuff her desk with dirty laundry."

"I'll b-bring my brothers' boxer shorts," Prairie volunteered.

We all went, "Eeoooh" just as Max climbed back on board. She cradled a tattered dictionary in her arm. As she clomped past, she stopped suddenly, opened the flap of the book, and removed a pistol. She aimed at Lydia and began shooting.

Lydia screamed.

Max smirked. "It's only water." She replaced the water gun in the carved-out dictionary and resumed her place on the beanbag chair.

Lydia swiped at her forehead. She looked at her hand. "It's green."

Max shrugged. "You wanted green hair."

"Hey, Max, that's not a bad idea," I said, scootching to the edge of the couch. "We load up water pistols with colored water. Shoot-out at the O.K. Corral. And we can get all the Nikes, so Ashley won't know she's the real target." I added with a smirk, "We'll give them a reason to call themselves neon."

The Snob Squad hyena-howled.

Max reached into the pocket of her camouflage jacket. She removed three more pistols and tossed them to us. "I've been collecting these," she said. "I figured someday they'd come in handy."

Prairie examined hers. "I'm going to l-load mine with g-green Kool-Aid," she said. "N-nice and sticky."

"Hey . . ." A slow smile crept across my lips. "Vinegar. Nice and stinky."

That got our brains storming. Catsup, mustard, OJ, sour milk, KC Masterpiece barbecue sauce. I could eat that stuff with a spoon, and I have. By the time we left the Peacemobile, we had a new plan of attack. Sure, it was juvenile. It was lame. But no one would get hurt, and we wouldn't get arrested.

At the door Prairie stopped and said, "Now, h-have we thought the plan through?"

We all stopped, looked at each other, and shrugged. What could go wrong?

Chapter 8

I rummaged through my mom's boxed-up library in the basement. My quest: to find the thickest book in her throwaways. "Hey, Mom, can I have this?" I asked her while she loaded the dishwasher.

She arched an eyebrow at me. "You want to read *War and Peace*?"

"It's for extra credit," I lied. "To get my grades up." To get my appointment canceled.

She poured Cascade into the soap slot and beamed at me. "Leo Tolstoy was my first love, you know." She sighed. "Go ahead."

I wondered if Dad knew about Leo. On my way out I asked, "Do you think you'll ever want to read it again?"

She pushed the dishwasher's start button. "I doubt it." Over the roar of rushing water, she added, "If you like that one, there's a whole collection of Russian novels in the basement somewhere." She smiled at me with new reverence.

"Okay. Thanks." Like I'd ever get through chapter one. "Could you hand me a steak knife?"

Mom frowned. "You're not hoarding food in your room again, are you?"

I clucked. "Who me?"

While I sawed out the middle section of the book, I dreamed. I dreamed of catsup curls and gummy braids. Icky sticky lemon locks. Mustard oozing down Ashley's neck. I thought I'd gotten over what she'd done to me. That I'd forgotten and forgiven. Now I knew I'd done neither. I hated her more than ever, and she was finally going to pay.

Operation Green Hair worked perfectly — in the beginning. Every couple of minutes one of us Snobs would open fire on a Nike. Prairie was out of lime Kool-Aid at home, so she had loaded her gun with Welch's grape juice. It made really cool purple streaks all the way around Melanie's blond sausage curls.

Max filled her gun with beer, I think. None of us had the guts to ask. But when it hit Fayola's head, it foamed. Lydia selected Grey Poupon. What else? Her pistol was stashed inside this trashy romance novel called *Love in a Limo,* which seemed appropriate—don't ask me why.

I kept my concoction simple. Sugar water. It was colorless and odorless, and as it dried in Ashley's ponytail, it hardened like cement.

What I didn't think about was how sugar water might cake up on the pistol after a while. How it might plug up the hole as the sugar crystallized. How it might shoot off target when I tried to shake it loose, and how it might squirt Mr. Krupps when he walked through the door.

"What the—" His eyes focused on the stream of liquid dribbling down the front of his pants.

"Nice shot, Solano," Max whispered behind me.

"See?" Ashley said. She appeared from behind her father. "Mrs. Jonas didn't believe me. But someone's got a squirt gun in this room. And they're shooting at me. Just feel my hair, Daddy. And smell it."

He sniffed. Everyone did. No doubt about it. Grey Poupon.

Immediately I slammed the cover closed on *War and Peace.* Mr. Krupps scanned the room with beady eyes. They screeched to a halt on me. Not on me.

Behind me. "McFarland, to the office." He thrust a thumb over his shoulder. "Mrs. Jonas, I'll see you during your planning period."

She blinked once. "Yes, Mr. Krupps," she said. Her eyes slipped down his wet pants. You could tell she was stifling a guffaw. As Mr. Krupps slammed out the door, though, Mrs. Jonas's amused expression changed to a scowl. And it was directed at Ashley Krupps, as if to say, "You little snitch."

Hey, what did she care? She was the principal's daughter. Ashley sashayed to her desk, nose in the air.

We learned at lunch that Max had been suspended. Prairie said, "There's only one C-christian thing to do—turn ourselves in."

So we all trundled off to the office.

Mr. Krupps didn't believe us at first. "She set you up, didn't she?" he said. "What'd Max do? Threaten you unless you confessed for her?"

"No," I replied. "We all have squirt guns. See?" We yanked them out in unison.

"Don't shoot!" He held up his hands. He must've realized what a nincompoop he looked like because he lowered them right away. Then his head began to shake from side to side. "Girls, girls, girls," he chided each of us. "I'm afraid I have no choice but to suspend you for bringing weapons to school."

Beside me, Lydia gulped the big one. I knew why. Her mother would have a cow. Not a Black Cow, either. She'd put Lydia on a lifelong behavior modification program.

I was kind of excited. No school. I could catch up on the soaps.

"We'll make it an in-school suspension for all of you," Mr. Krupps added.

Lydia exhaled a gale of relief. Prairie and I groaned.

Although in-school suspension always looked like fun—you know, permission to veg out for a day—it was actually quite humiliating. Delinquency is highly overrated. Mr. Krupps lined us up in adjacent desks along the wall outside his office. We weren't allowed to talk or whisper or even make eye contact. We weren't allowed to eat or drink. It was cruel and unusual punishment. Even if I'd had my stash with me, I couldn't have indulged because every couple of minutes Mr. Krupps sent his skinhead secretary, Mr. Terlitz, out to patrol the hall.

Once, just as I was about to faint, either from Terlitz's B.O. or the sudden plunge in my blood sugar level, a hand shot out and dropped something in my lap. A wedge of white paper. I unfolded it. One side was the multiplication work sheet we were supposed to be completing. On the other side was a note scribbled in pink ink. "My mom's going to kill me when she finds out," it said. "But I don't care. Poupon Ashley." A smiley face with green hair punctuated the pun.

I laughed. Terlitz whirled around.

"Sorry," I muttered. "Lost my mind. Have you seen it anywhere?"

Max snorted.

Krupps came out. "Mr. Terlitz." He halted him mid-lunge for my throat. "Do you have a copy of the school board agenda for tonight's meeting? I can't find mine." To us he snarled, "If I hear one more word out here . . ."

"Yeah, yeah," Max muttered.

Lydia whispered under her breath, "That's two."

Prairie giggled. I choked back a chuckle. Before we all dissolved into Looney Tunes, I snuffed out the sniggers with a stiff hand. "Sorry, Mr. Krupps. We'll get to work." If we weren't careful, we'd get expelled. Then, in addition to the shrink, my parents might send me to bed without dinner. Talk about a void.

Chapter 9

"**I** know where she lives," Max said as we thrashed through the junkyard toward the Peacemobile.

"Where who lives?" Lydia asked. We settled into our designated places.

"Mustard head," Max said.

It took Lydia a minute. "You know where Ashley Krupps lives? She never told *me* where she lives."

I knew where she lived. I never wanted to go back there again.

Max shrugged. "My brother sold her brother a rebuilt engine for his '87 Olds, and I went with him to help put it in." She thumbed behind her. "It's down a couple of streets from here on Quigley. That big brown and white house."

"Yeah, the giant Oreo," I said. "My bus drives by it every day." I used to love that house. It always got me hyped for my after-school snack. That was before. Now I get queasy when we pass.

"Are you ready to firebomb it now?" Max asked.

We all stared at her, considering. Even if Max knew how to make a firebomb . . . I shook the thought loose. "Why don't we just TP it?"

For a long moment all you could hear were the springs groaning under my weight. Then Max's eyes gleamed. So did Prairie's. Lydia said in a sigh, "I don't think my mom would let me go out after dark to TP a house."

"Would she let you out to firebomb it?" I asked.

Lydia sneered.

Max said, "Don't tell her what you're planning to do—" I know she wanted to add something like "wart head."

"I mean, I don't think she'll let me out at night, period."

That was a problem. Even if I had a Big Mac attack an hour after dinner, I couldn't go out alone at night either.

"Can't you sneak out?" Max said.

Lydia didn't answer. Neither did I. Confirming we were wimps.

Prairie said, "W-why d-don't we have a sleep-over or s-something? That'd be a g-good excuse."

"A sleep-over," I repeated. "Here at Max's. Brilliant, Prairie. As usual. Have a Tootsie Roll Pop." She selected grape from the open plastic package that I'd pulled from my backpack. Maybe in a group, maybe with a purpose, I could stand going near Ashley's house again.

"Sleep here?" Max's voice cracked. "At my house?"

"Sure," I replied. "We can all bring sleeping bags and spread out in your living room."

"No!" Max's face took on a shade reminiscent of Grey Poupon. "It's Friday night. We can't do it here. Not in my house. No way."

We all looked at Max. She just kept shaking her head and saying, "No way. Not tonight. It's Friday night." I wondered what went on in her house on Friday nights. Apparently it was something bad. Something she didn't want us to see.   aybe Friday was the night Scuzz-Gut Baggied up body parts.

Prairie piped up, "W-what about sleeping out here? In the van?"

We arched hopeful eyebrows at Max.

Her eyes darted around. "Yeah, I guess that'd be okay. As long as you didn't go in the house to go to the bathroom or anything."

We looked at each other. "No problem. We'll hold it. Right?" I was kidding, sort of.

Max said, "What do you do at a sleep-over anyway?"

Lydia scoffed. "You don't know?" She turned to me. "Tell her, Jenny."

My face seared fireball red. "How should I know? I've never been to a sleep-over."

Prairie piped up, "M-me neither."

I couldn't believe it. I thought I was the only one in the world who'd never been to a sleep-over. "Anyway," I said, "it's not a real sleep-over. It's a TP party. You eat and drink. Tell ghost stories. That kind of stuff."

"No ghost stories," Max said in that voice that made us cower.

"Okay," I said. "Then we'll just eat and drink. But we won't drink much, so we won't have to go to the bathroom." That seemed to relieve Max. I added with a smile, "And we'll plot revenge on Ashley Krupps."

"Yeahhhhh," Lydia breathed.

"Have another sucker," I offered.

We all got permission from our parents to sleep over at Max's, believe it or not. Even Lydia, although her mom had to call Max's mom to confirm and tell her that Lydia had asthma and if she had an attack not to worry, that Lydia would bring her inhaler. And that Lydia had to be in bed by nine because she had an early piano lesson the next day. "Blah, blah, blah," Lydia mocked her mother. "Sometimes she drives me crazy."

Which made me laugh. Then Lydia got the joke and laughed, too.

When I told my mom about the sleep-over, she started to cry. "Oh, Jenny." She hugged me. "How great." Like I'd never been to a sleep-over.

"So you'll cancel my appointment with the shrink?"

She blew her nose. "No."

Geesh, what did it take?

The plan was to bring as much toilet paper as we could stuff into our backpacks and sleeping bags. The TP supplies at home were running low, so on the way back to Max's I made a pit stop at Wal-Mart to pick up a twelve-pack. Angel Soft, my TP of choice.

Max told us to wear black, which made us look like terrorists in training. Which we were. My black sweat suit was a bit snugger than I remembered, but it was the only black clothing I owned. Lydia wore a black leotard with tights, plus a black ski cap with all her hair tucked up inside. It looked like she had a brain tumor. Which could explain her personality, or lack thereof. Prairie showed up in an old Halloween Dracula costume that she'd dug out of her brother's closet. Max wore authentic black and brown guerrilla warfare camouflage fatigues.

Just as we were rearranging furniture and rolling out our sleeping bags, there was a knock on the side panel. Beside me, Max tensed. "Who is it?" she said.

"Your mother," a husky voice replied.

Max got up and slid the door open. A woman, about half Max's height, stepped up into the van. She was dressed all in black, too. A black silk blouse over a full-length skirt. With a turban wrapped around her head. There was something strange about her. Strange and mesmerizing at the same time. Her eyes drew me in. They were bright, bright blue. "Are you going to introduce me to your friends, Maxine?" She smiled.

Max mumbled our names. Her mother shook each of our hands. She had very long fingernails, painted pale blue. "Are you coming to the gathering tonight?" she asked.

Max answered, "No, Ma. We've got stuff to do."

"Oh." She seemed disappointed.

My curiosity was piqued. "What gathering?"

Max shot me full of eye bullets. I didn't care.

"The spiritual gathering," she said. "My Friday night séance."

Séance? Whoa.

Max looked like she wanted to crawl into the carburetor and combust. I don't know why. I thought it was cool.

"Maxine did invite you, didn't she?"

Silence.

"Maxine." Her mother glared at her.

"Like I said, Ma, we've got stuff to do."

"Well, at least let me read your friends' cards. Come along, girls." She waggled a luminescent fingernail at us. "Let Madame Sibylique be your spiritual adviser. Allow her to answer your most burning questions."

Boy, did I have a few of those!

Lydia whispered, "I didn't bring any cards. Nobody told me you had to bring cards to a sleep-over."

I gave her a withering look. "We're not playing Old Maid."

"Madame Sibylique, your spiritual adviser," Max said sarcastically, "is going to read your tarot cards." You know she wanted to add, "tumor head."

Cool, I thought. Way cool. I love psychic stuff.

Reluctantly Max followed us out. From the end of the procession, loud enough for the heavens to hear, she hollered, "We are *not* staying for the séance, Ma."

Her mother twisted her head and smiled all-knowingly. "Yes, dear."

Chapter 10

Max elbowed her way through the kitchen to block the doorway to the back. A gauzy gray curtain covered the entrance. "We can do it here," Max said. For some reason she didn't want us going into the living room. It sure made me want to go into the living room.

Madame Sibylique sighed. "If you insist, dear." She pulled a pack of cards out of her skirt pocket. They were wrapped in red silk, and as she uncovered them she asked, "Who wants to be first?"

We all raised our hands. Lydia said, "Okay, Prairie. You're first."

That earned Lydia a sharp elbow from me. She elbowed back.

Madame Sibylique motioned Prairie to the kitchen

table. She sat down across from her and handed her the pack. "Please shuffle your cards," she said. "While you're shuffling, concentrate on your hopes, your fears, your dreams and desires. Think about the question you would most like to have answered."

Prairie nodded. You could tell she was concentrating hard.

We didn't have to ask our questions out loud, which was a relief to me since mine was, Will I marry Kevin Rooney and live happily ever after?

Madame Sibylique laid out ten cards for Prairie. After she studied them a minute, she smiled. "It appears that your question concerns love."

Prairie blushed. Madame Sibylique said, "This card, the Four of Wands, shows the coming of romance and harmony. The Ace of Cups says that you will be abundant in all things: Love, joy, and fertility."

Fertility? Immediately I changed my question to: Will I fill my void? Or maybe, What is my void and could I fill it with an Eskimo Pie? Is that two questions?

Lydia said Max could go second. Just to be ornery to me. Max didn't want to go, so Lydia and I scrambled for the chair. She won. I considered flopping on top of her and giving her a hernia, then changed my mind. Who could stand to hear her scream?

First thing Lydia did was drop the cards all over the floor. Typical. After Madame Sibylique laid out the cards, she studied them for a long time. All the while she kept murmuring to herself, "Uh-huh. Uh-huh."

Uh-huh, what? Did Lydia deserve a hernia?

"Lydia," she said at last, "it seems you are struggling against opposing forces. An inner force and an outer one." She pointed to the card directly opposite Lydia. "This card means you are facing a choice of vital importance. See how it's reversed?"

I leaned over to get a good look at the upside-down card. It was called the Fool. Behind me, Max snorted.

"You must be careful not to make the wrong choice," Madame Sibylique added. "There are dire consequences. Also, you appear to be experiencing some parental difficulties."

"No kidding," Lydia said.

That surprised me.

"But," Madame Sibylique said with a smile, "this card is strength. The triumph of love over hate. Yes, your strength and courage will see you through."

"Sweet," Lydia said.

Strength and courage? Lydia? She must've mis-shuffled.

Finally, it was my turn. While shuffling, I concentrated on my hopes, fears, dreams, and desires. I didn't get too far beyond fears.

When Madame Sibylique laid out my cards, I heard Max exhale an "ooh" beside me. What? I looked at the cards. There were a bunch of sword cards. And one, the one closest to me, showed a skeleton with a bunch of swords sticking out of the bones in his back. It was labeled *Death*. Madame Sibylique gathered the cards back into a pack and said, "Why don't you shuffle again, dear?"

I did. And it turned up again. The Death card. Madame Sibylique "hmmmed." She "hmmmed" again. The hmmming went on longer than Lydia's uh-huhing. "Your question seems to be about something you are missing. Something you desire."

My void. My eyes widened at her. She was good.

"I see many obstacles to fulfilling your heart's desire," Madame Sibylique began.

Max muttered under her breath, "Yeah. Misery, suffering, loss, and defeat."

Really? I glanced up at Max. She averted her eyes.

Just as Madame Sibylique was getting to the Death card, the front doorbell rang. Max jumped a mile. She crunched two cockroaches on her way to the back door. "We gotta go now, Ma."

"All right. Just a minute. Jenny," she said, "you will succeed in the end. I do see victory."

She and Max exchanged a look. I didn't like the look of it. Madame Sibylique gathered the cards up quickly. Too quickly, I thought. Max reached across the table and grabbed the back of my sweatshirt. "Come on. Let's get out of here." Her grip tightened like a noose around my neck as she yanked me up.

Outside, the smell of rotten garbage bit my nose. Something furry skittered across our path, and Lydia yelped. She and Prairie charged for the van. While they climbed in, I broke away from Max and pulled her aside. "What did my cards really say?" I asked her.

She glanced back at the house, then gazed off across the junkyard. "It's a bunch of baloney," she replied.

"Baloney. Salami. Just give it to me straight, Max."

Max exhaled a long sigh. "You're never supposed to tell the bad cards. . . ." She paused. "But yours were pretty bad."

"Did they really say misery, suffering, loss, and defeat?"

Max didn't answer. Or maybe her silence was the answer.

"What about the Death card?" I had to know.

Max shook her head. "Just forget it. It doesn't mean hooey."

But I couldn't forget it. Misery, suffering, loss, and defeat? Plus the Death card, all in one sitting?

"That was so f-fun," Prairie said when we clomped up into the Peacemobile.

Lydia added, "Yeah, your mom is fantastic."

Max slammed the van door. "You want her? Take her."

We all looked at Max.

"She's a fake, okay? She thinks she's this whoop-de-doo channel to the spirit world, that she can predict the future and communicate with the dead. She takes people's money, then makes up all these stories. She's a liar and a cheat, okay? So don't tell me how great my mother is."

The three of us exchanged glances before our eyes hit the floor. Poor Max. My mother embarrassed me; she made me mad, too. For instance, this one time I overheard her tell my grandma she wished I was more like Vanessa. That Vanessa was such a perfect child, so trouble-free. My mother is deep into denial, but I didn't think that made her immoral. It was Lydia who said, "Your mom and my mom are a lot alike. My mom thinks she knows everything about everybody. They say one word and she analyzes them to death. I don't even want to bring my friends home." She stopped and shook her head. "Let's not talk about mothers."

"G-good idea."

Even if Max's mom was a phony, I was still trying to shake off the creeps from my tarot cards when Max held out an opened jar to me. "Here," she said. "This is for your face." She scooped out a glob of purple goo and smeared it on her cheeks.

It had a tantalizing aroma. "What is this gunk?" I taste-tested it off my thumb. "Yum."

"Blackberry jam," Max said. "I was going to use axle grease, but it doesn't wash off too good. This was the darkest stuff I could find."

Lydia made a face at me.

"She's the expert," I explained.

Once we were all smeared up, I looked around the group and made an observation. "We look like Tootsie Roll Pops."

Prairie said, "My f-favorite, too. G-grape." We all cracked up.

Max slid open the door panel. She hesitated and

spun around, focusing on me. "Maybe we should forget this."

I knew it! She believed. She believed the tarot.

"Forget it?" Lydia wailed. "I've been waiting all my life for this. Don't chicken out on me."

Wrong thing to say to Max McFarland. Her eyes narrowed. Her fists clenched.

I jumped in. "Yeah, let's forget it. Let's go to the séance instead."

Max glared at me. She jumped down and snarled, "Come on, then. Let's get it over with."

I assumed my bad karma would show up later in life. That it'd appear little by little. And that it wouldn't extend to my friends. Wrong, wrong, and really wrong.

Chapter 11

With thirty-three rolls of toilet paper jammed into three backpacks, we slithered stealthily into the night. As stealthy as a motor-mouth, a dragging Dracula, a kamikaze commando, and a hooded hippopotamus can be.

The sky was sneak-attack black. No lights were on at the Krupps's house as we approached from the north. It gave me the willies to be near this house again. And on Friday night, too. The street was only dimly lit by a fluorescent lamp at the corner, until we hit the Krupps's driveway and a bejillion watts of electricity illuminated the entire block. "Geez," Max wheezed. "Get down."

We scrunched to our haunches and crawled back

behind a lilac bush out front. The driveway spotlight blinked out after a couple of minutes.

"It's one of those motion detector lights," I whispered. "My dad just put one in over our garage."

"Great," Lydia mumbled.

"Let me have your hat," Max said to her. Lydia handed over her ski cap. Max jammed it onto her head and ordered us to stay put. Like a jaguar, she sprang out of the bush and charged toward the garage door. The spotlight flashed on, showing every puzzle piece in her camouflage field jacket. She vaulted the picket fence to the right of the garage and ripped the ski cap off her head. In a single bound she covered the light with the hat. Immediately it grew dark again. Not axle-grease black like I would've preferred, but dark enough. At least you couldn't see the whites of our eyes.

Max raced back, breathing hard. "Let's go." She unlatched one of the backpacks. Lydia grabbed a fat roll of Scott tissue and sang, "Geronimo!"

Lydia charged out into the yard and tripped. She called back in a whisper yell, "Watch the hose."

You could definitely see the whites of Max's and my rolling eyes. Lydia hauled back and launched the toilet paper over the roof, where it disappeared into the night.

We snuck up behind her. "Why'd you do that?" I said.

"I thought that's how you did it."

Max piped up, "You have to hold one end when you throw it. Like this." She unfurled a roll of flow-ered TP, held one end, and tossed the other up into the maple tree out front. The bottom square of tissue tore off in her hand, while the roll wedged about halfway up the tree in a branch. "Crud," Max said.

That's two wasted rolls, I thought. Aloud, I whis-pered, "I'll decorate the front bushes and the porch area."

Prairie said, "I'll h-help."

As we divvied up rolls between us, I heard Max grumble, "How do you get it to hang down in the trees?" and Lydia say, "Here, you hold one end and I'll run with it."

A siren blared. Like missiles, we launched for the lilac. It was some other crime on the next block over, probably a drive-by shooting, but my heart was ham-mering a hip-hop. As I yanked a couple more rolls of Charmin out of the pack and thundered toward the porch, a car turned down Quigley. Its headlights captured me in the act.

I hit the deck, knocking Prairie into the rosebushes, then landing right on top of her. She "oomphed" as the car sped by.

"Sorry." I helped Prairie up. She was okay, but the roses weren't. Flat as French toast.

We went through all thirty-three rolls of TP in about ten minutes, which felt more like ten years with the dogs barking and doors slamming and sirens wailing. Whoever called it the dead of night was deaf as a Ding-Dong.

Racing back up the block, we paused behind an RV to admire our work. From the wash of streetlights on the corner, we surveyed the damage. "Not bad," I said. "For amateurs."

It wasn't bad. Toilet paper draped like thick cobwebs all over the yard, shrubbery, trees, and mailbox. Yes, the black widows had snagged their prey.

That night I had a nightmare. A sword cut through the black curtain of night, and it was dripping blood. Ashley Krupps's blood. Right in front of me, she collapsed. Like the picture on the Death card, there were swords sticking out all over her back. Blood pooled around her body. Then it wasn't Ashley anymore. It was me, my body. I woke up suddenly, nauseated and sweating. My sleeping bag was soaked. For a long time I just lay there, thinking. Thinking about my cards. About misery and suffering, loss and defeat. I felt as if I'd already experienced all four. Because of Ashley—what she'd done to me. The Death card was a mystery, though. Except for my beloved Petey, no one had died in my life. Afterward, after the Ashley incident, I wished I was dead. Did that count? Somehow I didn't think so. Could the Death card relate to what we did tonight? I didn't see how. TP'ing Ashley's house was just a prank, right? No one got hurt. Whoever died from a TP job? Stupid. But for some reason I couldn't stop shaking.

In class on Monday, everything seemed normal. During silent reading, Ashley passed a secret note to Fayola, who unwrapped her third stick of gum and shoved it into her mouth before reading the note. In front of her, Rachel Cagney braided Melanie's hair, while Melanie giggled at some joke Kevin Rooney made across the aisle.

The calm was driving me to drink. I finished off

both boxes of Hawaiian Punch from my lunch. When Ashley got up to sharpen her pencil, I jumped up after her. I hadn't spoken to Ashley all year, but I had to know. Since I couldn't avoid passing Mrs. Jonas's desk on the way, I casually mentioned to her that Fayola was chewing gum.

"Fayola, trash." Mrs. Jonas pointed.

Fayola snarled something colorful under her breath as she stormed past me. I stuck out my tongue. I know, kindergarten.

While Mrs. Jonas resumed her reading, I glanced at Lydia and Max. They both shrugged. Neither had heard a thing about our dastardly deed. It was weird. Maybe I was sweating blood sugar for nothing.

At the pencil sharpener, I swallowed back bile and said to Ashley, "So, anything exciting happen over the weekend?"

She looked at me like, You talking to me? Jenny Solano, sewer sludge? Words are flowing from your lizard lips to my esteemed ears? She finished grinding her glittery pencil and blew off the shavings. "They started putting in the pool at our new house," she said.

I wanted to bust her in the chops so bad. I wanted to . . . Pool? I hadn't seen a pool at her house. But then, we weren't in the backyard. A smile tugged the corner of my lips. I wondered if a fat roll of Scott tissue was floating in the deep end.

Ashley returned to her desk. Weird. I shrugged at the Squad.

Before lunch we stopped by the PC lab to pick up Prairie. When we got there, she was waiting for us and looking as green as the school's goulash. "W-we're in b-big trouble," she said. "We're all g-going to die."

Prairie wouldn't, or couldn't, say what she knew until we were alone. As we lined up for hot lunch, she whispered, "J-just act normal. Eat lunch."

No one has to tell me that twice. As soon as we were snarfing cheeseburgers, Prairie whispered, "I heard a r-rumor." She glanced over one shoulder, then the other. "T-Tony said his cousin Mario's house got TP'ed over the weekend, and he's out to g-get whoever did it."

"Tony Reese?" Lydia yelped. Prairie pressed a finger to her lips. My stomach plunged. Tony Reese was the brother of the leader of the Crips.

Could be a coincidence, right?

Lydia said, "Could be a coincidence, right?"

Max looked at me. I gulped.

For a long time we chomped our cheeseburgers in

silence. Then Max said, "Come to think of it, Tony's cousin lives on Quigley Street. My brother sold him a '66 T-bird hood ornament. I thought for sure his house was the orange jobby up the street from the brown and white one."

Then it struck me, what Ashley had said. "Oh, my God," I breathed. Everyone turned to me. "Ashley moved. She said they were digging a pool at her 'new' house."

After a prolonged silence, during which the only sound you could hear was the chewing of our last meal, Lydia said, "I hope we didn't leave any incriminating evidence at the scene."

Max choked. Her hand flew to her head.

"Oh, great." Lydia dropped her jaw. "We're dead meat."

"It was just a b-black cap," Prairie said.

"Right," I added quickly. "No one can trace it back to Lydia." I looked at her. "Can they?"

Lydia swallowed hard. "My mom might have painted my name in it. She's into puffy paint."

Slowly, a vision materialized in my brain. Swords. Blood. Death. Max met my eyes. She saw it, too.

The rest of the week was a blur. Not only did I fear for my life, but for the Squad's safety by association.

At least twice an hour I reviewed my life. It was a short one but a sweet one. I didn't want to see it end. Not like this. Not lying in a pool of blood. You know how blood makes me woozy.

The relay races only fueled my fear. I kept looking over my shoulder, waiting for the Crips to appear. Gun me down on the final turn. I raced for my life, literally.

By Wednesday, when we were all still alive, I breathed a little easier. Maybe the Crips had forgotten. Maybe they'd given up their life of crime to sell, say, a line of designer clothing. Leather and chains. Bullet bracelets. Stuff like that. Just when I was feeling full of hope, Ashley pulled the plug.

As I lined up at the starting post, the Nikes jumped off the bleachers with Ashley yelling, "Wait, Mr. Dietz. Don't start yet." She was hiding something behind her back.

Fayola stood in front of the gym teacher. In a loud voice, loud enough for everyone to hear, Fayola announced, "We want to make sure the Snob Squad's times are up-to-the-minute accurate." She motioned to Ashley.

On cue Ashley whipped out her cache. It was a wall clock, one of those big round ones from the hallway. "You'll need the hour hand to time Jenny's leg," Ashley said.

Everyone howled. Even Mr. Dietz struggled to keep a straight face. I lost it.

I lunged like a grizzly for Ashley's throat. At the point of impact, Max stepped between us. Blocking my flailing fists, she forced me back. "You get an automatic suspension for fighting," Max said.

She should know.

Little by little, my temper cooled. I whirled in place. To the Squad I snapped, "Peacemobile. Now."

"Now?" Lydia said. "But school—"

I lumbered off the field toward the clown target. My lardo legs picked up speed. Faster and faster, I charged for Erie Avenue and leaped off the curb. In my blind rage, I never saw the bus that hit me.

Chapter 12

If you're thinking the same thing I was, that I was finally dealt the Death card, you're wrong. I didn't die. I woke up in the hospital with my mom and dad hovering over my head.

"Oh, Jenny." Mom kissed my face.

Dad squeezed my hand. "You're lucky to be alive," he said.

"Am I?" I had a headache that registered off the Richter scale.

Mom said, "What kind of question is that, 'Am I?'"

Honest, I answered to myself.

"Do you remember what happened?" Dad asked.

"I fell?"

"Right into an oncoming bus," he said.

"Really?" My eyebrows arched. "Did I total it?"

Dad shook his head sadly. "'Fraid so."

"Good. Was it my school bus?" I hope, I hope.

He didn't get a chance to answer because the door opened and a nurse bustled in to check my vital signs.

After she left Mom said, "What were you doing, running out in the street during gym class?"

"Escaping," I replied.

"From P.E.?"

Was that a joke? Did Mom actually crack a joke? I almost laughed. Instead I said, "No, from the aliens. Don't you see them? They're everywhere."

Mom blinked across at Dad. "She's kidding," he told her. "Or maybe not. She has suffered a major head trauma."

Mom muttered, "Thank God I got that psychologist's appointment when I did."

That bolted me back to reality. "I have to go to the bathroom," I said.

Mom and Dad both helped me up. When my feet hit the floor, my head exploded. "Did I have brain surgery?" I asked. There were no bandages. Apparently they left the speech center intact.

"You have a concussion," Mom said. "The doctor wants to keep you overnight for observation."

The way I felt, he could keep me for suffocation.

Dragging my corpse across the room, I didn't notice her until I got to the bathroom door. Vanessa stood stock-still, staring. Not at me, at the wall. Or what was on the wall. A mirror. Lately, she had this thing about mirrors. She got lost in them.

"Vanessa? Jenny's awake," Mom said as we passed.

No response.

"Vanessa!"

Vanessa flinched and turned her head. "Jen." She threw her arms around me. "Oh, Jen."

"Don't squeeze," I said. "I have to go."

She released me. "Are you okay? Does it hurt?"

"Only when I breathe," I said.

"So don't." She sneered. A flicker of the old Vanessa returned to her eyes. But the flicker faded fast because she caught sight of herself in the mirror again and disappeared.

When I came out of the bathroom, everyone was getting ready to leave. "Get some rest," Mom said. "I'll be back in the morning to pick you up."

Dad tucked covers up around me. "Are you hungry? I'll have the nurse order you a meal."

Miraculously, I wasn't hungry. Food was the last thing on my mind. Maybe my appetite center had been surgically removed. "Order me two meals for the morning," I said in a yawn. Just in case.

He and Mom kissed me good-bye. They dug Vanessa out of the mirror and left.

No sooner had I figured out the TV remote control than the phone rang. It was Lydia.

"Oh my God, Jenny. How are you?" she said.

"Alive. Barely. I have a concussion."

"Is that all? I mean, that's enough. You're lucky to be alive."

Where had I heard that before?

"We were so worried," Lydia went on. "Especially when the ambulance came and took you to the hospital."

"I rode in an ambulance?" Rats, I didn't even remember. "Bet that was exciting."

"No kidding. Everyone was screaming and crying. Even Ashley."

"She should cry," I said. "It was all her fault."

Lydia babbled on for a while about how the bus screeched to a stop, but not before it dragged me under. How it swerved and crashed into the clown target. How Bozo was smashed to smithereens, and how Ashley ran screaming to the office to call 911.

"Oh, sure. She probably called the PTA so they could sue me for blitzing Bozo," I muttered.

I must've drifted off, because I woke up the next morning thinking it was all a dream. When they brought in my breakfast tray, I realized it was a nightmare.

Oatmeal. Gag. I hate that stuff. And *two* heaping bowlfuls. Dad was true to his word. Just as I lifted the phone to dial Domino's for a pizza, the lights went out.

"Surprise!" The Snob Squad leaped around the corner. Well, Lydia leaped. Max and Prairie sort of shuffled in.

"What are you guys doing here? Shouldn't you be in prison?"

Max smirked. "Probably."

"We got the day off," Lydia said.

I looked at her. "You mean you ditched?"

She grinned.

"Your mom's going to kill you."

"So what?" Lydia said. "We had to see you. They wouldn't let us up without an adult, so we snuck in."

"How do you f-feel?" Prairie asked. She clenched the bed rail. "We thought for s-sure you were dead."

"No such luck."

Max clucked. "Anything busted?" she said.

"Just my head. I get out today."

They all exhaled in relief. Max elbowed Lydia. "What?" Lydia said.

Max growled at her.

"Oh, yeah." Lydia unzipped her fanny pack. "We brought you a present." She pulled out a bag of Tootsie Roll Pops and shook it over the bed.

"You guys are the best," I said. "Rip that sucker open."

While everyone chose a flavor and unwrapped a sucker, I made room for them to sit on the bed. Max pulled up a chair instead and rested her army boots on the rail. Out of the blue Lydia said, "Are you ever going to tell us why you hate Ashley Krupps so much?"

It froze me mid-slurp. Out in the hall a cart rolled by and a beeper sounded. Max got up and shut the door.

They all waited. How long could they wait? Their silence was making me mental. "Okay"—I took a long lick—"here goes. I had this friend, Zoe. Zoe Zarlengo?"

"I remember her," Max said. "Long, thick braid. Like an Indian." She motioned down her back.

I winced at the memory. "Right. The rest of you

wouldn't know her since you didn't go to Abrams Elementary. Anyway, Zoe and I were best friends in fourth grade. Zoe was the best friend I ever had." I removed the sucker from my mouth and added, "The *only* friend I ever had." A lump lodged in my throat. Just thinking about Zoe made my heart ache.

"So what about Ashley?" Lydia said.

"Shut up." Max scootched her chair closer. "She's getting there."

"Fifth grade started out good," I said. "I mean, I hated school. It's not easy for a fat girl, you know? I wasn't as fat as I am now, but I was overweight. I always have been. I was born fat. Like a birth defect." What a stupid thing to say. My eyes met Prairie's, and she nodded understanding. Thank goodness.

Max said, "You're not fat."

I said, "Lydia, give Max your glasses."

Lydia clucked.

Max said, "You should see my uncle Mel, you want fat." She puffed out her cheeks.

I could've kissed her. Probably not a good idea. "Anyway," I went on, "at least school was bearable with Zoe there. She always defended me. Stood up for me if somebody said something mean, which happened about six times a day. She ate lunch with me. If we had to pair up for stuff, she picked me." The lump grew to a lemon and wedged in my esophagus. I coughed. It wouldn't budge.

Prairie handed me a glass of water with a straw. After I sipped, she took it back and held it.

My throat hurt, but I forced myself to continue. "Right before spring break Ashley decides to form this secret club. The Sacred Circle of Sisterhood."

"Oh, brother," Lydia said. "I can guess what happened. She asked Zoe to join and not you."

"No, she asked both of us, which was a shocker. But there was a condition. This certain thing you had to do to be voted in."

Lydia gasped. "You had to strip in front of everyone?"

Where did she get this stuff? "No, but close. You had to reveal a secret. Not about you, about a friend. You had to prove to the other sisters that you trusted them with your life. Whatever you told them would go no further than the sisterhood because everyone was sworn to secrecy."

Lydia clucked. "And Ashley told?"

Max said, "She's getting there. Shut up."

"Stop telling me to shut up," Lydia snarled.

Max flinched. "Okay, put a lid on it, Lydia." She smirked. Lydia whapped her. "Go on, Jenny."

Without even getting to the chewy chocolate center, I stuck my sucker stick side up in a bowl of oatmeal. It was too hard to talk and lick. And there was such a sour taste in my mouth anyway, a sweet sucker was a waste. "I thought the club was a stupid idea, but Zoe wanted to join," I said. "She had this fatal flaw. She wanted to be popular. So we accepted the invitation. One night, a Friday night"—it made me queasy just to remember—"we were both asked to come to Ashley's house to meet with the sisterhood. To be interviewed. It was really spooky. Ashley led us downstairs to the basement. All the lights were turned out, and there was black construction paper over the windows. A card table was set up in the middle of the room with a candle burning on it. Three other people sat around the table. They wore sheets over their heads so we couldn't see who they were."

"Like devil worshipers," Lydia breathed.

"No doubt. Ashley asked us both to wait in another room while they got ready. It was the laundry room, which, if you've ever been alone with a washer and dryer in the dark, you know how creepy that is."

"I d-do," Prairie said. "Once when I was little I g-got locked in the laundry room." She shivered. "I thought for sure the b-boogeyman would jump out of the dryer and g-get me."

"The boogeyman would've been better than Ashley Krupps," I muttered. "She asked Zoe to come out first. Zoe was gone about an hour, or at least it felt that way. I couldn't hear much, just some muffled giggling. When Zoe came back, she was smiling. 'Don't do anything I wouldn't do,' she said. I remember that now. Oh, God." I covered my face with my hands.

An orderly whooshed through the door to retrieve the breakfast tray. "You didn't eat much," he said. "Not hungry?"

"Not crazy," I mumbled. "Help yourself."

He looked at the oatmeal with the sucker stuck in it and made a face.

"It just grew there," I said.

After the orderly left, Lydia gripped my leg through the covers and said, "Tell us the rest."

"Ow. Okay, don't get a hernia." I exhaled a long breath. "Where was I? Oh, yeah. The sisters sat me in a chair and made me hold out my palms. Then Ashley dripped candle wax on my wrists."

"Ouch. Didn't that h-hurt?"

"It hurt like crazy. I still have a scar." I showed

them my right wrist. "Ashley recited some chant, then told me about the initiation rite. About the secret. She said Zoe had passed. That she'd revealed a secret about me, and that I should tell one about her. That surprised me. I didn't remember telling Zoe any secrets. And I didn't want to tell what I knew about Zoe. She was my friend. But . . ." I stared off toward the bathroom wall. I wished Vanessa was there. Maybe she could show me how to lose myself in the mirror.

"But what?" Lydia shifted on the bed and bounced my head. The headache roared back with a vengeance.

I looked at Lydia, at the others. In a small voice I told them, "But I didn't want Zoe to be in the club and not me. You know?"

"Of course we know." Lydia patted my kneecap. "Go on."

I gulped. "I only knew one secret about Zoe. So I revealed it." Time stopped. The room whirled.

"What was it?" they all said at once.

I widened my eyes at them.

Max shook her head. "You don't have to tell us if you don't want to."

"No, I want to. It doesn't matter now, anyway."

Suddenly my stomach hurt. It felt like knives were in there, stabbing at flesh. That, plus the sore throat and the headache. Where was a doctor when you needed one? Close to convulsing, I continued, "I told them Zoe's real name was not Zoe Zarlengo." A moment passed to let them take that in, to let my heart begin beating again, before I added, "That's all I said—at first. But of course Ashley needed to know Zoe's real name. She said if I wanted to join I'd have to tell the whole secret. To prove I trusted the sisters."

"So you did," Lydia said.

"Yeah. I told them Zoe's name was Kayla Ferguson."

The Snob Squad exchanged confused looks. "I don't get it," Max said. "So what?"

"Ashley wanted to know why Zoe was using a false name. She wouldn't let it go. She kept badgering me. Finally I told her the truth. I didn't know. All I knew was that it was this big secret and I promised never to tell."

Prairie asked, "So w-what happened?"

I said, "Ashley must've figured out the reason. And she must've run right upstairs after we left and told her father about it, too, because the cops were at Zoe's house by the time we got there. What's worse is, on the way home, Zoe said she made something up about me. She said I had a twenty-two-year-old boyfriend and we were going to elope. No one believed it until she showed Ashley a picture of her brother and me together. Oh, man." Tears welled in my eyes.

Prairie handed me a Kleenex. I blew my nose. "I never saw Zoe again. I found out later that her mom was hiding her and her brother from their dad. They'd been running from him for years. She must've guessed what I did. I never even got to explain. I never got to say good-bye." The last word came out a squeak because a torrent of tears burst through the dam. They'd been storing up for a year, and now they all flooded forth.

The Snob Squad just let me cry it out. Lydia patted my leg the whole time.

Once I'd wadded up an entire box of hospital Kleenex, Lydia said, "Ashley Krupps is a snake."

I sniffed. "If she ever tells you she's sworn to secrecy, just stab her in the back. Like she did to me." Tears threatened again.

Max stood. "Tonight. Peacemobile. Sleep-over," she said. "We're gonna kick Krupp's butt from here to kingdom come."

Lydia and Prairie both nodded agreement.

I had no idea where kingdom come was. But those were the words I'd been longing to hear. I looked around and thought, I love you guys. I wish I could have told them.

Chapter 13

The Snob Squad left right before Mom showed up to bring me home from the hospital. That afternoon I had a lot of time to think. Usually I can veg out in front of soaps all day when I'm home sick, but today I couldn't put the brakes to the brain. I relived the whole Ashley incident, even the end, when I felt so guilty. When I knew in my heart I'd betrayed Zoe. Even if Ashley had held a gun to my head, I should never have revealed Zoe's secret. What are friends for if you can't trust each other? Trust is a precious bond. You can't form a club. You can't pledge trust.

During a commercial for Kraft macaroni and cheese, the big revelation came. It wasn't Ashley's fault. She didn't hold a gun to my head. She didn't force me to say a word. I should've known not to believe her. I should've gone with my gut instinct, especially when Ashley said she was sworn to secrecy. The only thing Ashley Krupps is sworn to is building herself up by tearing others down. She always has. She always will.

It was my fault Zoe went away. My fault. I missed her. I miss her still. The worst part is wondering where Zoe is now, how she's doing. Wondering if she's found a new best friend. Knowing Zoe, she has. She was such a great person. I just hope her new best friend is a better friend than I was.

Mom said I could go to the sleep-over as long as I took it easy. What I took was a box of Eskimo Pies.

Handing them out, I said to Max, "I know I didn't exactly die, but do you think I've experienced enough misery, suffering, loss, and defeat?"

Max just clucked.

"What are you talking about?" Lydia said.

I explained about my tarot cards. About the swords. About the Death card.

"The D-Death card?" Prairie shuddered.

"It doesn't mean death," Max said. "At least not physical death. The Death card only means a change of consciousness. Like death of the old self and rebirth of the new." At my awed expression, she shrugged. "So I know how to read tarot cards. So what?"

"It could mean physical death," Lydia said. "It could mean we should firebomb Ashley's house."

"We don't know where she lives," I said. "And even if we did—" I stopped and took a deep breath. This was risky, I knew. "Let's just forget it."

"Forget what?" Lydia said.

"Forget about taking revenge on Ashley Krupps."

"What!" Lydia squeezed her Eskimo Pie, and it plopped out of the wrapper onto her lap. While she wiped it up, she said, "You mean just forget all the mean and horrible things she's done to us? Not get back at her at all?"

"That's exactly what I mean."

"But she lied to you. She almost got you killed! She made you get hit by a bus."

We all let that ring in our ears. It sounded stupid, even to Lydia. You could tell by the red in her cheeks.

"I ran into the street," I said. "I got hit by the bus. And I betrayed my friend Zoe. Don't get me wrong. I hate Ashley Krupps, but I think it's a waste of time to keep thinking up ways to get her. Nothing's going to change. She sure isn't."

"But we'll feel better," Lydia's voice rose an octave.

"Will we? Okay, I admit, it was hilarious seeing the Nikes all sticky with mustard and beer hair. But who got in trouble? Us. And who's on the Crips' hit list for TP'ing Tony's cousin's house? Us. And who ended up with a concussion and almost died? Us. I mean, me. But you could've been right behind me. Face it. We're lousy at this."

"I think that concussion cracked your skull," Lydia muttered.

"Yeah," I said. "It cracked open my head and let a little sense in. Listen, every time we do something mean to the Nikes, we're just like them. And I don't want to be like them. I especially don't want to be like their leader, Ashley Krupps. We're better than that. Aren't we?"

No one answered.

"Well, aren't we?" My eyes circled around the Snob Squad. They all gaped at me, wondering, I'm sure, whether they should call the hospital and have me readmitted. On the psycho ward. It was no use. I figured I'd been wrong abut them. "Would you buy just as good?" I mumbled as I got up to leave.

Prairie said, "N-no. We're better."

I turned back. "You bet we are. Anybody want another Eskimo Pie?"

Lydia scowled. "So what do you suggest we do,

Jenny? Just let them get away with it? Let people like Ashley Krupps keep on humiliating us forever?" Her voice edged toward a screech.

"No," I replied, handing her a pie to calm her down. "We're not going to put up with any more crap. What we need is a new attitude. You said it, Lydia. You called us the Snob Squad. Maybe we should act it. Allow me to demonstrate." I pushed up my nose with my index finger and strutted across the Peacemobile. Prairie covered her mouth and tittered. She jumped up and copied me, and pretty soon Max was doing it. The Snob Squad Salute.

Lydia met my eyes. She wasn't convinced, I could tell. This was hard for her. But maybe, like her tarot cards said, she had to make a choice. Finally, reluctantly, she rose and joined us.

Our troubles weren't over. We knew that. If it wasn't Ashley and the Neon Nikes, it'd be somebody else tormenting us. We were targets. But we didn't have to be easy targets. Maybe, if we banded together, we'd make moving targets. And if we kept moving, we might just make it through middle school.

My appointment with the psychologist was Saturday morning at ten. Since I couldn't persuade Mom to cancel the appointment, I devised a plan. I called it the "Jenny Solano Dummy Up Plan to Frustrate the Head Fed." My best role was playing the Blob. I looked the part. No one dared mess with my body, and no one was going to mess with my mind, either. Not even a trained professional.

Mom picked me up at Max's, looking a little shocked over where I'd spent the night.

"Don't worry, Mom," I assured her. "We only drove the van to McDonald's and back."

I guess, seeing the tires on the Peacemobile were flat as Fruit Roll-Ups, she recognized the humor.

The shrink's office was on the twenty-third floor of a glass and marble skyscraper. Even though we were rising up, up, up, I felt my stomach plunging down, down, down.

The office had Mickey Mouses stenciled all over the walls. Appropriate, I thought.

"Hello, Jennifer. I'm Dr. Sidhwa." A short, dumpy man came out to greet me. He extended a hand to shake.

I let him waggle my limp wrist. The way he said Jennifer, so exotic sounding, made my scalp tingle. He said hello to my mother and ushered me in. My eyes strayed over my shoulder. I wanted Mom to come with me so bad. She smiled encouragement.

"You can call me Dr. Sid." He pronounced it Dr. Seed. "Do you have a nickname?" He motioned to me to sit.

"Blubber Butt," I said, taking the only chair. There was no couch or else I would've sprawled out for a nap. It'd been a late night.

He smiled. "I'll just call you Jennifer."

"Jenny," I said. If my scalp tingled too long, I might let down my guard. He had kind eyes.

"Jenny. Your mother tells me you have a problem."

I rolled my eyes.

He folded his hands. His fingers were short and fat, like Vienna sausages. "Do you think you have a problem?"

"Yeah," I said. "My mother."

He chuckled. "Don't get me started on mothers." He threw up his hands. "Mine calls me twice a week to ask if I'm engaged yet."

"Are you?" I said.

He pointed a fat finger. "Don't you start." Smiling, he settled back in his chair. "Tell me about yourself. You're in sixth grade, yes?" He arched an eyebrow.

Okay, I thought. Time to implement the Plan. I just sat there. In a second he'd start to squirm. He'd fill the empty space with speech. A second went by.

Then fifteen, twenty seconds. This was getting uncomfortable. How long could he stare at me, eyebrows arched?

He won. I couldn't stand it. "I'm fat," I said. "So what else is new?"

"Is this new?" he asked.

"No. I was born fat. Not this fat. But then, I wasn't born this tall either."

Dr. Sid smiled. He studied me. "How long have you been this . . . weight?"

"I don't know. A year. Do you watch *Oprah*?"

"What?" He frowned.

Oops, I cringed. It might be against his religion to watch tabloid TV. Even though Oprah was tasteful tabloid.

"*Oprah*. You know, the talk show? Never mind."

"Yes, I know *Oprah*. I do watch her occasionally. I like her."

"Really?" That surprised me. "Well, Oprah says if you overeat it's because you have a void in your life. And she should know. She's weighed like two hundred and forty-three pounds."

"She doesn't look overweight to me."

"No, because she found her void and filled it. With money, is my guess."

He laughed. "What's happened to you in the last year to create this void?"

"What hasn't happened?" I stopped. The last year. The last year had been lousy. Talk about misery, suffering, loss, and defeat.

"Would you like to tell me?" Dr. Sid said.

If I didn't, he'd stare me down again. My exhaled stream of breath came out long and low. Why not? "I had this friend, Zoe Zarlengo. . . ."

It wasn't nearly as difficult to tell the story the second time. Of course, he got an abbreviated version. I didn't reveal names or dates or places. Nothing incriminating. Nothing important. Nothing deep down.

"It's very hard to lose a friend," Dr. Sid said at the end.

"Especially a best friend. I mean, I had Petey, but he died on Halloween."

Dr. Sid's eyes widened.

"He was my hamster."

"Ah." He looked relieved. "I imagine you loved your hamster."

"Yeah, I did," I said. "Even though he was just a hamster, I had him since I was nine."

"So you lost two friends in one year."

I nodded. "And the only other person I was ever close to was my sister, and she flipped out last summer." Oh, my God! It all made sense. That summer after Zoe left, Vanessa started losing touch. Not just with the world; with me, too. Then Petey died. Zoe, Vanessa, then Petey. All gone. "You're good," I said to Dr. Sid.

"Excuse me?"

"Three friends," I said. "I lost three friends in one year. I mean, that's enough to create a void in anyone's life, isn't it?"

"Definitely. So you believe your void is a lack of friends?"

"Oh, no. I have friends. I mean, I do now. Three friends." Which was kind of ironic, wasn't it? "Hey, I think my void is filled," I said, standing. "I guess I'm cured."

He clapped his hands together. "Wonderful. Perhaps we need to talk a little more. Would you mind?" He indicated the chair.

"Do you give out lollipops at the end?"

"What?"

"Nothing. I guess since you don't have anyone else's life to save for an hour." I shrugged and sat back down.

"Now," he said, leaning forward over the desk, "let us go back a minute. You say your sister flipped out. What do you mean she flipped out?"

I cozied down into the soft leather upholstery. This was going to be an extended session.

Afterward, Mom met me in the waiting room. "So, how'd it go?" she said.

I slipped into my backpack. "Good."

She gave me that look—you know, details? As we walked to the elevator, she asked, "What'd you tell him?"

I smiled at Mom. "Everything. Next week he wants to meet with Vanessa."

Chapter 14

"**Y**ou know, making us get weighed in public is psychologically damaging. We're very sensitive about our bodies at this age. And I should know. My mother's—"

"Her mother's a child psychologist," I finished for Lydia. "Believe what she says."

Droopy Dietz sighed. "Is there anything about life that isn't psychologically damaging?" He looked at Lydia. "Don't answer that. Okay, if it'll reduce the mental anguish, I'll move the scale into the office. But people, I need to get your heights and weights for the next phase of the fitness test."

As we herded toward the office door, I inched my way to the back. Talk about mental anguish. The last time I'd weighed myself I experienced one of

Vanessa's psychotic episodes. Dizziness over the digital readout.

Prairie said, "At least you're t-taller than me. And my prosthesis weighs a t-ton."

"Thanks, Prairie." I smiled meekly. Wish I had something to blame my tonnage on.

Ahead of us, Ashley stomped out of the office. "The scale's broken," I heard her say to Fayola. "It weighs at least five pounds heavy."

"Oh, great," I muttered. That'd put me over the top. That'd jam the works.

Sweat was streaming down my sweats by the time my turn came. Terlitz the Terminator, who was doing the honors, asked my full name and birth date. I was tempted to give him false information, but prior consequences with fake names nixed that notion. "Okay, step up onto the scale," he ordered.

I did, then jumped off. "Wait," I said. I kicked off my shoes and peeled away my socks. Tiptoeing back on, I exhaled my last breath. "Okay. Shoot."

He adjusted the little metal indicator. Up, up, down a notch. No warning sirens sounded. Terlitz scribbled on the form attached to his clipboard. "That's it," he said. "Get down."

That's it?

Here's where you're going to confirm your suspicion about my sanity, or lack thereof. Here's where you're going to agree with my mother that I do indeed need professional help.

I said, "So, how much do I weigh?"

He pursed his skinny lips at me. "You really want to know?"

No, I want Ashley Krupps to know so her father can announce it to the whole friggin' school. I shrugged. "Why not?"

He showed me the form. My kneecaps disintegrated. When I stumbled out, the Squad waited in the wings. Lydia grabbed my arm. "Jenny, are you okay? You're white as a ghost."

Ghost. That was a good word. I was a ghost. A ghost of my former self. "I lost six pounds," I said.

"All right!" Max held up a palm and I smacked it.

"P-plus five," Prairie said, "if Ashley's right about the s-scale."

Hey, yeah. I decided to believe Ashley Krupps was telling the truth, just this once. Eleven pounds. "I don't know how this happened," I said, slowly shaking my head.

"I do," Lydia said. "You've been sharing all your candy with us—that's how."

I looked at her. She might be right.

"Okay, folks, I have a few announcements," Mr. Dietz said. "Could we rally round?"

In slo-mo we all shuffled over to the tumbling mats. "First," he said, "I have the results of the relay races." He consulted his sheet.

We all zoned out, or at least I did.

"Best overall time, the Oakland Raiders." I applauded, to be polite. I wished it'd been Kevin Rooney's team since I'm deeply in love with him. He came in second. "Worst overall time," Mr. Dietz paused. He caught Lydia's eye and sighed.

Oh, great, I thought. More public humiliation. More suffering, more defeat . . .

"The Neon Nikes."

There was a loud intake of breath in front of us. Ashley wailed, "That's impossible!"

"'Fraid not," Dietz said. "You girls missed two races. I had to give you zeroes. I don't know what was so all-fire interesting up there in the bleachers, but I didn't think it was my responsibility to come up and drag you down for your heats."

"They were probably plotting to get us," I whispered to Max. She smirked. Lydia heard and snickered.

"And you kept droppir the baton, too," Melanie said to Ashley.

"I did not."

"Did, too. And you never let me run the last leg. I'm the fastest," Fayola said.

"You are not!"

"She is, too," Rachel jumped in.

"That's enough," Dietz cut them off. "You'll have a chance to make it up in this next phase. And, let's see. Most improved time: the Snob Squad."

"What!" we all cried together.

"Yes," Max cheered. We high-fived.

I couldn't believe it. Then I could. I mean, we started out as slow as Saskatchewan. Where is Saskatchewan? Canada, right? Anyway, with Max's encouragement (or threat of execution by the Crips), we must've picked up speed.

"The next phase will be strength building," the Dietzman said. "You can work in your same teams."

Melanie raised her hand. "Do we have to? I don't want to be on Ashley's team anymore," she said.

Rachel said, "Neither do I."

Ashley slashed them dead with machete eyes. She turned the fire on Fayola. Fayola said quickly, "I think we should switch. Mix up the teams."

I raised my hand. "I think we should keep the same teams. It'll be a lot easier to keep track of, paperwise."

The idea appealed to our gym teacher, you could tell. "You're right," he said. "We'll keep the same teams."

Max and Prairie smacked palms. "Wait a minute." Lydia waved her hand in the air. "I think we should change."

I looked at Lydia. My spirits sagged. I thought for sure she was with us, that she'd made the right choice.

She said, "I think we should keep the same teams but be allowed to change leaders. We want our team leader to be Jenny Solano."

My face flared a fire stick.

"Sure, sure. That'd be fine," Dietz said. "Can we get started now?"

"When did you decide this?" I whispered while Dietz droned on about how to use the weight training equipment without injuring ourselves or others.

"While you were in g-getting weighed," Prairie said.

"It was unanimous." Lydia smiled. I looked at Max. She slugged my shoulder. Good thing I still had some fat reserves left.

Leader? Me? Suddenly I felt different. Changed. As if the old me had died and a new me had been born. A vision materialized in my mind. The Death card. Maybe this is what Max meant by a change of consciousness. A death and a rebirth.

"Jenny, snap out of it." Lydia snapped her fingers in front of my face.

"Must be the concussion," Max said.

"P-permanent brain damage."

"You guys." I waved them away. "All right, as your newly elected commander-in-chief, my first duty is to inform you that Sunday is my birthday. You are all invited over Saturday night for a sleep-over. That's an order, not a request."

Max clicked her army boots together and saluted. "Yessuh."

Prairie and Lydia saluted, too. That made us all collapse into hyena hysterics. Ashley stormed past and snapped, "Shut up."

We all did the Snob Squad salute, finger to nose to Ashley. She just sneered and stomped away toward the principal's office. Strange. I didn't hate Ashley Krupps anymore. At least not as much as I used to. I felt kind of sorry for her, if you want to know the truth. Ashley was just being Ashley. I forgave her for that. Someday I might even forget.

My last thought, before the whole class got put on notice was, This is going to be the best birthday I've ever had. Between the four of us, we might eat enough cake to fill my void. To fill all our voids. Yes, I thought. Mow down misery, snuff out suffering, laugh at loss, defy defeat. Next year was going to be better. Sweet, as Lydia would say. Isn't that how revenge is supposed to taste?

Julie Anne Peters is also the author of *The Stinky Sneakers Contest*, *B.J.'s Billion-Dollar Bet*, and *How Do You Spell GEEK?*, as well as another book about Jenny, Lydia, Max, and Prairie, *Romance of the Snob Squad*.

Julie Anne Peters lives in Colorado.